The Second Coming

Judgement Day

Paul Georgiou

Published by Panarc International 2024
Copyright © Paul Georgiou, 2023

First Edition

www.panarcpublishing.com

Panarc International Ltd
www.panarc.com

ISBN Print: 978-1-7395472-3-3
ISBN Epub: 978-1-7395472-4-0
ISBN Kindle: 978-1-7395472-5-7

The Second Coming
Judgement Day

Contents

I.

Surprise

Monday

"**D**READFUL day," observed James Cleveland, the UK's 62nd Prime Minister. The two vertical lines on his forehead above and between his eyes were unusually deep, indication of a medium level of irritation. He was sitting in his chair in the cabinet room. He liked to work there in preference to his own office. He found it more prime ministerial, probably because his was the only chair with arms.

"Are you referring to the weather or the news?" enquired Archie Kildare, Chief Adviser to the Prime Minister.

Kildare was not a typical civil servant. Indeed, whether he was a civil servant at all remained an unresolved question. He had been recruited and appointed by the PM, circumventing all normal HR procedures, thus disconcerting the entire civil service. His reputation as a maverick did little to recommend him to the inevitably complacent top level of administrators. His substantial wealth acquired while working for five years in the City, combined with his sybaritic lifestyle, put the final touches to his image as a *bête noire* of a generally conservative establishment. That both he and Cleveland had studied at the same Oxford College (though not at the same time) and, according to the *Daily Mail*, were distantly related was for many in the chatterati the last straw.

"I was referring to the weather," Cleveland replied, frowning. "Why, is the news particularly dreadful?"

"You mean apart from the unending fractious trade negotiations with the EU, the flare-up in the Middle East, the deterioration in our relations with China and the rumour that another pandemic is on its way?"

"Yes, that's what I mean," Cleveland replied, a little testily.

Archie Kildare grinned. "Well, there's a spontaneous demonstration heading towards Number 10, even as we speak."

"What do you mean a 'spontaneous' demonstration? Any demonstration has to be cleared with the Met."

"Well this one hasn't been," Archie responded. "It's an anomaly as demonstrations go, as indicated by the adjective 'spontaneous'."

"How big is it? How many people?" Cleveland asked.

"I'm told its about five thousand."

"What! Are you telling me that five thousand people have spontaneously gathered somewhere and decided to march on Number 10?" Cleveland was now both alarmed and angry. "What the hell do they want?"

Archie Kildare abandoned his mildly jocular tone. Clearly the PM was not in the mood for levity. "We aren't entirely sure," he replied. "There's the usual ragbag of semi-professional demonstrators but they're in a minority. The majority don't fit any of the usual demonstrator categories. There are well-dressed, middle-class individuals marching alongside manual workers and elderly hippies. A very odd mixture. They certainly don't seem to be extremists of either the left or the right. As for what they want, it's difficult to tell."

"You're exceptionally ill-informed on what is clearly an unusual and possibly dangerous situation," Cleveland rebuked his adviser. "Are they carrying any banners? Are they chanting any slogans? Banners and slogans might just give us a hint of their demands."

"Nothing like that," Kildare explained. "They seem good-humoured. There's no shouting. And certainly no anti-social behaviour. In any case, the police are on it. They'll hold them at the entrance to Downing Street. We'll find out more when the Head of the Met reports to you. She's at the gates now. She'll brief you as soon as her people have talked to the demonstrators."

James Cleveland grunted. "What's happening in Palestine? Have the Israelis annexed any more land?"

"No," Kildare replied, relieved that the PM had changed the subject. "Apparently the allegations of corruption against the Israeli Prime Minister have thrown into doubt the survival of his coalition. He may not be in office by the end of the week."

"And the rumoured pandemic?"

"It's another virus originating in China," said Kildare. "The Chinese government has banned wet markets, but the people are ignoring the ban. I ask you, what's the point of having a ruthless, one-party totalitarian state if you can't make people do what you want?"

"Do we know the virus has come out of a wet market?"

"No, we don't have definitive proof of its origin. Yet again it seems to be a toss-up between a local wet market or a bat cave in Yunnan Province. As usual we have the benefit of China's open book information policy, so getting to the truth is almost impossible."

"Really?" Cleveland decided his Chief Adviser was rather too chirpy. This was, after all, 9 a.m. on a Monday morning of what promised to be an exceedingly challenging and trying week. "Really?" he repeated. "You thought the last one escaped or had been released from the Wuhan Institute of Virology. As my adviser, you really shouldn't speculate about the cause of such important matters as pandemics. You should be keeping me up to date with the facts so that I can take informed decisions. Let's take the impending invasion of Downing Street as an example. If you could tell me who the hell they are and what the hell they want, I'd be in a much better position to decide what the hell to do about it. Do you see what I mean?"

Kildare didn't reply immediately. It was clear the PM had risen from his bed on the wrong side that morning.

"As I said, PM, the demonstration appears to be entirely spontaneous," Kildare offered defensively. "There were no reports of plans for a demo today, so it has taken everyone by surprise. Rest assured, you will be the first to hear the Commissioner's report."

There was a buzz. Cleveland answered the phone. "Send her in," he said.

2.

The very model of a modern police commissioner

JULIET Money was the quintessence of the new breed of police officer. While maintaining an essential core of steel in dealing with career criminals and terrorists, she was, truth to tell, more at home in emphasising the social causes of crime – that was, poverty and lack of education – both of which obviously lay outside the responsibility of the police.

"Hello, Juliet," said Cleveland, and then, without giving her a chance to sit down, added, "What the hell is going on?"

"They want to talk to you," she said.

Cleveland was not a patient man. "They want to talk to me. Hmm! Now let me see. Let's say I give each of the five thousand demonstrators ten minutes. That would be fifty thousand minutes, so I should be able to complete the task in about twenty weeks. Let's say five months. Just to save a bit of time, I don't suppose you have any idea what they want to talk about? And they don't by any chance have a leader or a small group of leaders that I might talk to – that is, if there is any conceivable reason for me to talk to any of them at all in the first place?"

"I have ordered them to disperse," said Juliet. She had a conflicted relationship with Cleveland. She hadn't made it to the top of the police force without a strength of character and a determination that could easily withstand Cleveland's sarcasm. And his discourtesy irritated her. On the other hand, he was good at his job and knew how to get things done.

Cleveland shook his head to indicate incredulity, the furrows in his brow deepening. "Then why are we having this discussion? If they have no demands and if they are dispersing, surely we are wasting our time."

"I didn't say they have no demands PM. They want to speak to you. That is a demand, if you like. And I didn't say they were dispersing. I said I had ordered them to disperse."

"Are you telling me that they're not dispersing?"

Cleveland asked in a tone implying that if she answered yes, an incisive critique of the Police Commissioner's authority would follow.

"They say they are waiting for someone," Juliet replied, "before they disperse."

Cleveland's eyes narrowed. "And who is it they are waiting for? An audience with me, or for someone else? Their leader, perhaps? An articulate spokesperson who has some really constructive ideas on how to run the country – or some rabble-rousing moron who's managed to inspire a few thousand idiots to march in support of his eccentric, hare-brained and completely impractical cause?"

"They are not waiting for an audience with you. When I said they want to talk to you, I meant that they want the one they are waiting for to talk to you on their behalf."

"So it's probably the rabble-rousing moron," Kildare suggested helpfully. "We certainly don't want an articulate spokesperson with constructive ideas on how to run the country. That's my job."

Cleveland ignored his Chief Adviser's contribution. "Who is it? Who is it they are waiting for."

"I don't know," Money said, clearly embarrassed. "No one in the crowd can give me a name but they're all agreed someone is coming and that person is going to talk to you."

"Well, it's high time you disabused them of their

conviction that I'm prepared to see any Tom, Dick or Harry just because he's managed to persuade a mob to embark on an illegal march on Downing Street."

Juliet Money could see that Cleveland was angry. She knew what would come next. He would question her competence. He would probably say that while she was very good at explaining the causes of crime in terms of dozens of governmental failures to address social issues, when it came to fulfilling the primary function of the police, namely ensuring the law was obeyed and order was imposed, she was rather less effective. She'd heard it all before. And if necessary, she would listen to it again. But not in front of the supercilious, unelected tosser Kildare. So she took pre-emptive action.

"With your approval, I will order armed police to issue a warning that if the crowd does not immediately disperse, I will authorise lethal action."

Kildare laughed. Smart move, he thought. *Evidently, I've misjudged her. And not at all bad-looking either, in a blue-stocking sort of way. I've always had a leaning towards women in uniform.* "Not even a couple of warning shots?" he enquired innocently.

"I was rather hoping you would be able to deploy the natural authority that goes with your office," Cleveland said coldly, "before mowing down dozens of peaceful, unarmed demonstrators."

"With respect, PM," said Juliet Money, uncowed by Cleveland's rebuke, "we govern with the consent of the people in this country. I have a simple choice when dealing with an incalcitrant mob – I can beg, or I can shoot.

"I'm sure you can find a happy medium between the two extremes – perhaps exercising the authority that goes with your role as Police Commissioner," Cleveland suggested, his patience, never thick to begin with, wearing very thin.

"May I respectfully suggest," Money said, undeterred, "you are forgetting the bloody-minded attitude embedded in the English character, the antagonistic response to any orders that can be construed as an infringement of what are conceived by the masses to be their inalienable personal rights."

"Juliet, just get it done," said Cleveland. "Try arresting a few. If that doesn't work, you have my permission, not that you need it, to bang a few heads. We'll keep the armed police out of it for now."

"I will try, of course, PM," said Money, "but when you take into account recent cuts in the police budget and the totally inadequate police establishment, we have to be careful. We don't want to start a fight we can't win." Money intended to elaborate, providing statistics on the reduction in budgets and manpower of the previous decade, but James Cleveland interrupted.

"Just get it done. Now."

3.

Cabinet meeting

FROM Cleveland's point of view, the cabinet meeting had gone well. Fred Tyler, the Foreign Secretary, and Andrew Purdy, the Home Secretary, were, as ever, jockeying for position. If they put as much effort into running their departments as they did into knocking chunks out of each other, then the country's domestic and foreign affairs would be in much better shape.

Trade negotiations with the EU were as fractious as ever. "Negotiating with Brussels is like swimming through porridge," Tony Bulmer, the Minister for Trade, and a man much given to metaphors, had complained. "They could find a nit to pick on a bald head," he had added.

The Foreign Secretary had taken time out from his jousting with the Home Secretary to report that if Israel attempted to annex any more Palestinian territory, Iran was prepared to back an unprecedented wave of terrorist attacks on Israel. He added that there was some evidence that China would not be unhappy if the Middle East tore itself apart. It would further undermine the United States, which would have to support Israel at a time when it was desperately trying to disengage from the region, and it would take the pressure off China, whose record of abuses of human rights was becoming a serious obstacle to its ambitions to achieve pre-eminence on the world's stage. "Then there's the issue of water rights," Tyler had added. "I predict that competition for water will prove to be a more contentious and intractable problem than the Arab/ Israeli conflict."

"How did it go?" Kildare asked when Cleveland returned to his office. Although he was the PM's Chief Adviser, he was not permitted to attend cabinet meetings.

"As usual," said Cleveland. "The Middle East situation is worrying. If there is a major conflict, apart from the human suffering, the oil price will go through the roof and the global economy will take a battering. But if you're right about the Israeli PM going down for corruption, there might be a window of opportunity for diplomacy.

According to Fred, we should be at least as worried about water. He reckons that's even more likely to cause trouble in the region in future."

"In that event, we can count on Fred to pour oil on it," Kildare quipped.

"What's happening with the mob?" Cleveland asked. "Has Juliet got rid of them?"

"Not exactly," Kildare replied. "The one they were waiting for has arrived, and she's told them to go home."

"It's a woman?" said Cleveland.

"So it seems"

"And has she been told to go home?" Cleveland asked. "Has she been told that she can't just walk into Number 10 and demand an audience?"

"Probably best if the Commissioner explains," suggested Kildare. "She's waiting for your call."

"Then get her in."

4.

Arrest the woman

JULIET Money entered the PM's office and sat down.

"I'm delighted to hear the crowd has been dispersed," Cleveland began. "I understand the leader of the mob is a woman. Who is she, what does she want and what have you done with her?"

Juliet seemed a little dazed. "She arrived on a horse," she said.

"She arrived on a horse?" Cleveland repeated.

"Yes, she rode up Horse Guards Road on a magnificent white stallion, dismounted and marched up to the gates of Downing Street," Juliet added.

"And was arrested," Cleveland suggested. "She was arrested?"

"Not exactly," said the Commissioner. "She ordered the crowd to disperse."

"I thought you ordered the crowd to disperse."

"I did," said Juliet. "But they didn't go. Then she told them to leave … and they did. And when they left and the situation was resolved, it seemed churlish to arrest the woman. After all, she had been very helpful."

"Am I missing something?" enquired Cleveland. "A woman on a horse encourages a mob to march on Number 10. Having made her point, she orders her followers to depart. And we're grateful?"

Juliet paused. "She said she hadn't asked anyone to march on Downing Street. Indeed, she seemed almost irritated by their presence."

"You're not making much sense," Cleveland responded. "Why did they march if not at this woman's bidding? You said they were waiting for her to arrive, so they knew she was coming. Doesn't that suggest to your incisive, investigative brain some kind of arrangement between the leader and her followers?"

Cleveland waited for a full half minute. Then he said; "Please tell me she's been charged with something – disturbing the peace, organising an illegal demonstration, riding a horse through the city, anything – and placed under arrest."

"It's not illegal to ride a horse through London," Kildare offered helpfully.

"Well?" Cleveland said to Juliet Money.

"I will arrest her, if that's what you want," said Juliet. "But I think you should see her."

Cleveland shook his head. He was angry and incredulous. He had a full schedule for the week, from 7 a.m. to midnight, all seven days. A host of domestic issues required his attention, and on the international front, there were troubles in every direction. On top of that, Emma, his wife, was about to start the second stage of chemotherapy. "I don't think so," he said quietly. "I will not see her. Have her arrested and charged. Ensure she has adequate legal representation. And then make sure Crown Prosecution hits her in the face with the heaviest book in their law library."

The meeting was over.

5.

Unarrestable

JAMES Cleveland had no time for a proper lunch. Instead, he took ten minutes out to sit in his office and eat a prawn cocktail sandwich. He put in a call to Emma to check on her medical treatment. He knew how draining chemo could be.

"I'm fine," Emma said. "No, really, I'm fine. You don't need to worry. I haven't started the second stage treatment yet. The doctors are discussing my case. They say it's purely precautionary." Typical of Emma, Cleveland thought, Emma telling him not to worry. Not telling him how much she must dread another round of chemo. No, not a word of self-pity. Simply reassurance for him: "Don't worry. I'm fine."

Cleveland had made quite a few mistakes in his life, but marrying Emma wasn't one of them. Whatever life threw at him, Emma had his back. And quite often she was out in front, dealing with threats and problems before they reached him. He owed a great deal to Emma. They hadn't had any children. That was his one regret, not so much for himself, but for her. She had always wanted a child but it just hadn't happened. They'd both been checked out. There was no physiological problem. There had been some speculation about a possible mismatch of blood types but nothing definitive and it just hadn't happened.

Archie Kildare sauntered into the PM's office.

"It's the oddest thing," he began.

"What is?" Cleveland asked, mildly interested.

"They haven't arrested her. They haven't arrested her because they can't arrest her," Archie explained. "She seems to be unarrestable."

"No one is unarrestable. That's why there isn't a word for it. What do you mean?"

"I went out with Juliet to watch her exercise her authority," said Archie. "When we stepped out of Number 10, there she was, the horsewoman. The police had let her through the barrier – without her horse, of course. Juliet seemed flummoxed and I could see why. The woman is …" Kildare was never usually at a loss for words.

"The woman is what?" Cleveland prompted. "Come on, man. Spit it out."

"The woman is … unusual," was all Archie could manage.

"In what way?"

"It's difficult to explain," Archie said, clearly struggling to answer. "It was clear to Juliet that she couldn't arrest her. It was clear to me that Juliet couldn't arrest her."

"You're not making any sense," said Cleveland. Given the start that morning, he was beginning to wonder whether he was going to make it through the week. "Why couldn't anyone arrest her? What happened?"

"She introduced herself," said Archie. "She has a beautiful voice – soft, low and melodious."

"For God's sake, get to the point," Cleveland exploded. There was something wrong with Archie. The Chief Adviser had the best brain of anyone Cleveland had ever met. He was astute, analytical and intellectually ruthless. Yet here he was, mooning over the voice of a woman who was disrupting governmental business, making a fool of the police and humiliating the Commissioner."

"Her name is Jess. And she said she's here to see you,"

"And I assume you told her I don't see people just because they want to see me. You told her that I'm a busy man, that as PM, I have quite a few important matters to deal with. You told her that?"

"She said that you would see her. She said that your meeting with her would be the most important meeting of your life. She said she hoped, she very much hoped, that you would not disappoint."

Cleveland laughed. "Is she insanely arrogant or merely insane? This is ridiculous. Why haven't you had her taken away. Or are you smitten? *She has a beautiful soft voice.* Has she by any chance got a beautiful face and body to go with it? I've always seen you as a cynical and ruthless seducer of innocent, naïve women. Surely you haven't finally met your match."

"No," Archie exclaimed. "It's not that. It's nothing like that. She is, she is …"

Cleveland waited.

Eventually, Archie managed to finish the sentence. "She is very sure of herself".

6.

Jess

WHEN the woman walked into his office, Cleveland immediately understood why Archie Kildare had found it difficult to describe her. Indeed, he was so struck by her presence that he failed to question how she had passed through Security and into his office without anyone informing him of her impending arrival.

"I have no name," said the woman standing before him, "but I understand you will feel more comfortable if I adopt one. I have chosen Jess."

"Please sit down," was all Cleveland could manage.

"You must be wondering why I am here in your office in London, rather than in the White House in Washington, or in the Kremlin in Russia or in the Great Hall of the

People in Beijing," Jess said calmly as she settled into a chair opposite Cleveland.

Cleveland had not been wondering anything of the sort. He was in fact struggling to accommodate this compelling woman in his mind. On his way to the top of the greasy pole in British politics, he had acquired and honed an ability to determine very quickly what people were, the key components of their nature and what they most wanted. He would judge one person to be ruthlessly ambitious, unencumbered by any moral sense; another to be wholly motivated by money; yet another, altruistic but entirely impractical. Although these were snap judgements based on a few minutes' conversation, most of which were taken up with introductions and polite formalities, his instinctive assessments had never been proved wrong.

And his instinctive assessment of Jess would be no exception – because he hadn't been able to make one. She was a good height for a woman, attractive in an imperious way, and she was black-skinned, with the fine chiselled features of some Somali women. Her most striking feature was her eyes, a brilliant green which seemed as though they were backlit. She had a good figure, strong but womanly. Dressed in a white trouser suit, she could have been a successful BAME businesswoman. Cleveland had no problem in taking in her physical appearance. What he couldn't assess – or as he would put it, "accommodate" – was her presence. As Kildare had observed, she seemed to radiate confidence.

"Well?" Jess said, inviting him to affirm his curiosity about her decision to prefer him over the leaders of the USA, Russia and China.

"I'm sorry," said Cleveland. "I'm afraid I didn't register what you said, but before I say anything, I have to ask, why are you here?" He then added, as he forced himself back to normality, "and how you managed to pass through at least three layers of security."

"How I am here is a question you should address to your own people," Jess answered quietly. "You seem to be obsessed with security. I've no doubt I am going to be a difficulty for your forces of law and order but that is inevitable. I am here to question your laws and surely challenge your concepts of order."

Cleveland looked at her quizzically. "Is that why you are here?" he asked slowly. He had assumed that the woman who had organised an illegal march on No. 10, was a political extremist of some sort, a single-issue individual on a crusade to impose her limited and intolerant view on others. Now he seriously considered the possibility that she was mentally unstable.

"That is not my purpose, but it is almost certainly an inevitable corollary," Jess replied.

"Then why *are* you here? What is your purpose?" he asked.

"It's not that simple," Jess replied. "I have come to ask for your help."

"My help in doing what?" Cleveland persisted. She was being evasive and he had a jam-packed schedule. He really didn't have time for this.

"That's the bit that's complicated," Jess replied.

"I see," said Cleveland. Then in a calm, controlled, prime-ministerial voice, he continued: "I'm going to send for my Chief Adviser. His name is Archie Kildare. I'm going to ask him to listen to you, find out who you are, what you want and then tell me. When he's finished cross-examining you, I'm afraid you will have to face criminal charges. You have organised an illegal demonstration and breached security here. I'm sorry but I'm extremely busy and you have already disrupted the smooth running of my office for long enough."

"I'm happy to talk to Archie Kildare," said Jess. "He's an intelligent, if rather frivolous, man and one on whom you rely for advice. I intended to enlist his support in persuading you to help me and I'm pleased you wish to facilitate the briefing I need to give him. As for your suggestion that I shall face criminal charges, in the fullness of time you will come to appreciate the irony of such a prediction."

As Cleveland pressed the buzzer to summon Archie, a number of questions were circulating in his mind. Was she mad, or at the very least delusional? Was she foreign? Although she had impeccable English, there was something odd in the way she used words and the cadences of her speech. Was she dangerous? She hadn't shown any signs of violence, nor had she made any threats, but she seemed coldly determined to have her own way, even when it was obviously impossible. How had she reached his office? Why hadn't the police arrested her? Why hadn't Security in No. 10 stopped her? Why hadn't his secretary called Security to have her removed?

No one answered the buzzer, but it didn't matter because as Cleveland buzzed for the third time, Kildare knocked on the door and entered. "Sorry for bursting in but your secretary isn't in the office."

"No problem, Archie," said Cleveland. "As you will see, Jess has managed to have her audience with me. I'm not entirely sure how she succeeded in circumventing all the obstacles that should have prevented her from reaching me, but no matter, at least for now. Jess and I have had an interesting conversation. It seems she wants my help. I'd like you to take her to your office and talk with her to find out who she is and exactly what she wants. When you have found out, I want you to report to me. I have warned her that when your conversation with her is over, she will have to face criminal charges. She seems unconvinced but we will deal with any misunderstanding when the time comes. Is that clear?"

Cleveland had delivered his account and his instructions in a matter-of-fact tone to keep Jess calm. At the same time, he hoped he had clearly indicated to Kildare that they were dealing with someone who was mentally challenged and, quite possibly, dangerous.

"Pellucidly," said Archie Kildare.

Kildare took Jess gently by the arm. She rose from the chair and went willingly with him. As soon as the door of his office was closed, Cleveland pressed the intercom connecting him to Security. By the time he had finished with them, the only security they would be concerned with was their own.

7.

Oh you of little faith

AS soon as they were settled in Kildare's office, each of them sitting in an armchair facing each other, Jess addressed Kildare: "You are a clever but superficial person. I am talking to you because, wisely or not, James Cleveland relies on your advice and I want you to advise him to do exactly what I say."

"Right," said Archie, ignoring the insult. "So what exactly is it you want him to do?"

"I want him to stop all the nonsense," said Jess.

"To stop all the nonsense," Kildare repeated. "Absolutely. But can you nail it down a bit? Which actual nonsense do you have in mind?"

Jess sighed. "All of it."

"All of it," Kildare repeated. "That's a pretty tall order." He still had no idea what she wanted.

"The tallest," Jess agreed. "Taller than God's order to Noah to build an ark."

"Wow!" said Kildare. He was wondering if reference to Noah was simply a vivid metaphor, or whether he was dealing with a smartly dressed, black-skinned, green-eyed religious fanatic. He didn't remain in doubt for long.

"I'm here to sort out mankind. I can do it by force, and I will if I have to. But I would prefer to use persuasion and for that I need help."

"*Sort out mankind*? Right. That's good. No one could argue with that. Very praiseworthy." He was flapping and knew it. "You mean, like, changing the course of history," he hazarded in desperation.

"Well someone has to – or history is going to come to an end fairly soon," Jess confided. "I'll be honest with you. He was all for closing everything down immediately and without warning. He said it would be the kindest thing to do. Obviously He's enormously disappointed. He's so disillusioned with humanity He just wants to be shot of you. It's not His most endearing quality. As you know, He's into Divine Retribution and He's impatient, which is odd, given He has all the time *in* the world and much more out of it." Jess seemed to be wandering off the point.

"By 'He' I take it you mean God," Archie hazarded.

"Who else?" Jess replied in a tone and with an expression that suggested Archie, never very highly-rated, had slipped a couple of notches further down her scale of respect for humanity.

"But how do you hope to change the course of history?" Kildare asked. For now, he thought it best to take her seriously. "We've got some really serious environmental problems – global warming, sea waters rising, desertification and a hell of a lot of political issues to deal with – the US and China are on a collision course, Russia resurgent, the Middle East, an ammo dump managed by chain-smoking arsonists. I don't want to be rude or in any way disrespectful, but what makes you think one unknown woman could have any impact at all on global affairs?"

"There you go again," said Jess. "You underestimated me last time, and now you're doing it again. And there's something else. This time things are different. This time I have permission to use all my powers. Last time, apart from a few miracles, I held back. I showed you the way and gave you the choice. This time, I'm not asking – I'm telling."

"So what exactly are you saying?" Kildare enquired. "And what do you mean by 'last time'?"

"And I thought you were the smart one," said Jess. "I am here. I am here. This is your famous, long-awaited Second Coming."

"Second Coming?" Kildare replied blankly. And then he understood. "*The* Second Coming." He paused and then it slipped out: "But you're a woman, and you're black," he said lamely.

"And you're pathetic," Jess snapped back. "Do you think the Godhead is bound to one sex or another? Do you think He has a preferred skin colour? I came last time as a man, with olive skin, brown eyes and dark hair. What's your problem with a black-skinned woman?"

Archie said nothing. What could he say?

"There's another far more important difference between then and now," Jess continued. "Last time, I talked of peace. I exhorted you to love one another. I told you to turn the other cheek. Well, that didn't work out so well. According to our records, since then you've killed millions of your fellow creatures, quite often in my name. So I'm back. But this time, as I said, I'm not asking, I'm telling."

"When I said you're a woman," Kildare replied nervously, "I simply meant that if you're truly the Second Coming, it would probably have been more appropriate, more credible, for you to assume the persona of a man, along the lines of Charlemagne, Napoleon or Nelson Mandela. That's all. Not denigrating women in any way. Oh no, siree. Total feminist, that's me. I'm not stupid."

"I see," said Jess, "so you're not stupid and I'm delusional. The same problem I had last time. Very few grasped the truth. Only the disciples believed I was the Son of God and most of them had their doubts. Even when I performed miracles, they doubted me. I've thought a lot about that over the years. I think it's probably because my miracles were all benign – healing the sick, raising the odd person from the dead, turning water into wine. Well, I've learned my lesson. If you want attention, it's best to be disruptive and destructive. I'm thinking earthquakes and volcanic eruptions. Just as a taster of what to expect this time round, I've dismantled your Communications and Security system."

"Really? And how have you done that?" Kildare asked warily. Obviously the only explanation was that the woman was mad, but she just didn't strike him as a lunatic. She sounded exactly as he would have expected the Son of God – or the Daughter of God – to speak if they had come back after a couple of millennia to sort things out. Kildare was not a religious man but he had read enough of the prophecies in Revelations to know that if there was a Second Coming, it meant Judgement Day.

"I willed it," Jess said in answer to Kildare's question. "Just as I can will whatever I want. I am the Scion of the Creator. What I will, happens."

"And just supposing that the security system has not been disabled, will that cause you to reconsider your claim to be the Scion of the Creator or the Daughter of God?"

"Oh you of little faith," was all Jess said.

8.

Communication problems

CLEVELAND pressed the intercom button connecting him to Security again. There was no answer. He was about to storm out of his office when he collided at the door with Fiona Longworth, his secretary.

"What the hell is going on? Why haven't you been at your desk?" he asked brusquely.

"Communications are down," said Fiona. "I've just been over to Security and all their systems are down too. They think the system has been hacked."

"Jesus!" Cleveland exploded. "I can't believe it. In this of all weeks. Get hold of Kildare. I want him here now."

"I'll fetch him," said Fiona.

Within a few minutes, Archie Kildare entered

Cleveland's outer office. Jess was with him. He left Jess with Fiona and knocked on Cleveland's door.

"I've left Jess with Fiona," he said on entering. "We need to talk."

"That's why I sent for you. Why have you brought the woman with you?" Cleveland asked. He had momentarily forgotten he had instructed Kildare to cross-examine her.

"Didn't have much choice," Kildare replied. "According to Fiona, all our Comms are down. I didn't want to leave Jess on her own in my office, and without Comms it's difficult to organise appropriate safety measures."

"It's difficult to do anything without Comms," Cleveland agreed. "I've got a conference call with Robert this afternoon at three. We must have the main system running by then, or at least the backup. You need to make sure this happens. I don't care what you have to do. I can't miss a call with the US President because I've got a problem with my broadband."

"Right," said Kildare, "I'm on it. But before I go, please give me a couple of minutes to tell you about Jess."

"Really?" said Cleveland.

"Yes, really," said Kildare. "She is quite something.

I talked to her for a few minutes and it became obvious that she's delusional, seriously delusional."

"Fine," said Cleveland. "As soon as we can get hold of Security, we'll have her sectioned and taken into care. Now please sort out the Comms."

"That's what I want to talk to you about. She claims she has disrupted our Comms."

Cleveland's smoky grey eyes, usually open and kind, narrowed. "What do you mean? Are you saying she's part of some terrorist plot? Have you checked her out? Are you saying we've been hacked? She's picked a great day for a terrorist spectacular. After my chat with Robert, I'm supposed to fly to Brussels for a crunch meeting on trade tonight."

"No, it's not terrorism," replied Kildare, and then, momentarily diverted from his point, said, "I didn't know you were flying to Brussels."

"It came up early this morning. Our team have asked me to fly over. There's a crunch issue on financial services and they want me to be there." Cleveland rubbed his forehead. He could feel a headache coming on. "If it's not terrorism, what is it? And how the hell has anyone cracked or hacked our security system?"

Kildare thought of giving a full explanation but feared Cleveland wouldn't give him enough time. "She claims to be Jesus. She claims this is the Second Coming," he said, presenting the essence of the story baldly.

"But she's a woman!" said Cleveland.

"That's exactly what I said," confessed Kildare, "and got a bollocking for it. She said God didn't give a toss about gender, or race for that matter – not that she actually used the expression 'give a toss'."

"Well, obviously she's insane," said Cleveland. "Do you think she's dangerous? You've left her with Fiona."

"She's not dangerous in the sense that a psychopathic mad person could be dangerous," said Kildare, "but in the sense that she says she can will whatever she wants and it has to happen. She's a little bit worrying – mainly because she said that to prove she meant business, she would take down our Comms."

Cleveland blinked. "Are you saying you believe she somehow disrupted our entire Communications and Security system simply through an act of will? Are you as mad as she is? What world are you living in? Isn't it more likely she's in cahoots with some spotty adolescent anorak who has found a way to break into our system and she's here to blackmail us? Or that she's working with somebody inside our security network, probably a Russian agent, and wants to damage our credibility with our allies? Or that she noticed a blip in our electricity supply and took a chance on a maverick prediction that just happened to come off? All these scenarios are a bit off the wall, but surely you can see they're a tad more probable than that she is the Son, or Daughter, of God and has chosen 10 Downing Street as the venue for the Second Coming?"

Kildare shrugged. "You asked me to cross-examine her and report back. That's what I've done."

"I wanted an assessment, not a trip into Wonderland," snapped Cleveland. "If you believe her, tell her to will the system back up. It will save us all a great deal of time and trouble."

"That would be a good test," Kildare conceded.

"I was joking," said Cleveland dismissively. "Go through to Security. Send a couple of guards so we can be sure she's suitably detained and restrained, and then put everything we've got into sorting out the technical problems. Where are you going?"

In the middle of Cleveland's list of instructions, Archie Kildare had walked to the door of Cleveland's office, opened it and invited Jess to enter.

"I'm afraid the PM is a little sceptical, despite my best efforts to explain the situation," Kildare said to Jess. "Could you possibly will our Comms systems backup? That should be sufficient to convince him."

Cleveland glared at Kildare. Humouring the poor deluded woman was one thing; delaying what needed to be done to avert a political disaster was another.

"It is easier to disrupt than it is to build. It is easier to destroy than to create," said Jess.

The expression on Cleveland's face obviated the need for words. *What did I tell you?* was as clear as if he had said it.

"But if it will settle the matter, I will do as you ask," Jess continued. "It will take a minute or two."

Cleveland shook his head. Kildare appealed for two minutes' patience. Within a minute the phone rang.

"That's encouraging," said Kildare.

Cleveland frowned. He picked up the phone. "Security here, sir. We're back up. We ran a couple of checks through the system, closed it down and rebooted. Not sure why we had a problem. We had a similar situation a couple of years ago. We'll track down the cause but I thought I'd let you know we're back in business."

"Thank God," said Cleveland.

"Very appropriate," said Kildare.

"It's pure coincidence," said Cleveland. "Come on, man. You're not seriously suggesting ..."

"I'm not suggesting anything," Kildare interrupted. "But you made a deal."

"What deal was that?" Cleveland asked sharply. "There was no deal. Now I must get on. I have a meeting with Fred before my conference call with Robert.

"I would like you to clear your diary for the rest of today and tomorrow," Jess interrupted. "And if possible, it would please me if you didn't discuss me as though I wasn't here."

"I'm sorry?" Cleveland said, astonished.

"I think Archie has told you that I am here to sort out the mess that you and your kind have created. To succeed, I need your help. I should make it clear that this is mankind's last chance. Your stupidity and arrogance, your greed, your avarice and your cruelty have turned a world of beauty into a chamber of horrors. You have even managed to damage the planet, damage it perhaps beyond repair. So if I need an hour or two, believe me, there is no better way you could spend that time than working with me to salvage humanity."

"Take her out of here," Cleveland said to Kildare. "Take her out before I lose my temper."

"Do you want her charged with anything?" Kildare asked.

"Well, you could start with bringing down the entire Communications and Security system of the executive branch of the UK government."

"I thought you didn't believe she could do any such thing," Kildare gently goaded.

"Just get out and take her with you. My head is splitting. Deal with her as you see fit."

"We shall meet again this afternoon," said Jess, adding with a smile, "When your headache has passed and you are in a better mood."

9.

Tea for two

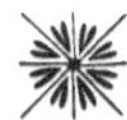

ARCHIE Kildare took Jess back to his office. "I'm impressed. Evidently you have the luck of the devil."

Jess looked at him, with a mixture of pity and irritation. "Do you mean I was lucky that your communication system came back online just at the right moment?"

"Well, yes," said Archie a little hesitantly.

"Or do you mean that a catastrophic fault in your system, which took out all your security, despite a couple of layers of backup, was resolved by a simple reboot?"

Archie frowned.

"Or do you mean that for the daughter of an ancient, primitive, tribal god now widely disrespected, I know far too much about how your technology works?"

Archie could see she was losing patience with him. He felt a little hurt. After all, he had used his influence with Cleveland to arrange a second interview, and for reasons he didn't fully understand himself, he had stood up for her. He had given her a chance to prove herself. "Would you like a cup of tea?" he asked.

"That would be good," Jess replied. "When I arrived, as soon as I dismounted, someone in the crowd gave me a beaker of tea. It was a strange but not unpleasant taste and refreshing."

Archie rang for tea. A pot and two mugs arrived promptly.

"You sound as though you haven't drunk tea before," Archie said with a laugh.

"You really are a bit thick," Jess observed. "*You sound as though you haven't drunk tea before*," she said, mimicking Archie. "I am the Scion of God. It's a long time since I had a body. And when I had a body, I don't think they had discovered tea, at least not in Palestine."

"Right," said Archie. "Sorry. Silly of me." If she's making all this up, she's obviously worked on her story, he thought, or she really believes she is the Second Coming.

"There is a third alternative," said Jess, as though she had read Archie's thoughts. "That I am what I say I am."

Archie was silent for a moment. Then he spoke. "You see my problem is that I don't believe in miracles. There is no way you could disable our Comms by an act of will. There is no way you could put it right with an act of will. There has to be some other explanation."

"And your other explanation is …?" Jess waited.

"Well, it has to be luck – or rather chance, a coincidence," said Archie.

"Really? So you prefer a non-explanation: it's just *chance*. Surely, since the Renaissance, you've believed that every effect has a cause. Yet now you prefer coincidence, or rather two coincidences."

"You like a good argument," Archie offered, hoping to take some of the heat out of the exchange. He considered adding that she looked very attractive when she was angry but thought better of it. It was most unlikely she would bring a case against him for sexual harassment, but nowadays you could never be sure. In any case, making a pass at someone who was convinced they were Jesus in a trouser suit was almost certainly blasphemous and possibly a little bit perverse.

"What have you got against miracles?" Jess asked suddenly. "You're surrounded by them. It's a miracle that there is a universe. Nothing is much more likely than something and yet something is everywhere. Life itself is a miracle. There wasn't any life for billions of years. Then there was. That's a big miracle right there. Then there's humanity. Out of the dust came Beethoven's Ninth, and Michelangelo's Madonna of the Stairs, and quantum physics. It's a miracle that the present somehow seamlessly manages to weld yesterday to tomorrow. Chaos is much more likely than order, but there is order. It's a miracle that effects have causes. It's a miracle that there are laws of physics. It's a miracle I rose from the dead. It's a miracle I've come back. Everything's a bloody miracle."

"Wow!" was all Archie could manage.

10.

Doctor's orders.

IN the White House, there was a flurry of activity. President Robert M. Haywood, 48th President of the United States, was unwell. He had just returned from his early morning jog when he fainted. The Vice President had been summoned as a precaution.

"I'm fine," the President had insisted. "It's probably something I ate. Probably the lobster thermidor last night."

"Sure you're right, Mr President," said the President's doctor, "but we have to do some routine tests. At your age, with the pressure of the job, you have to take care of yourself."

"Come on," Haywood said. "What do you mean *at my age*? I'm in my prime. In any case, I've got a call with

Cleveland scheduled for 7 a.m. That's in twenty minutes."

"I'm sorry but you'll have to cancel," said the doctor firmly.

"I can take it, if you like," the Vice President offered hopefully.

"No, no," said Haywood. "I need to discuss this Israel/Palestine issue. James and I have a good working relationship. I need to get him on board."

The Vice President, Hank Allbright, accepted the snub. He had no idea what the President had in mind but he'd been in politics long enough to know that any US meddling in the long-running Israeli/Palestinian conflict was fraught with dangers.

"You can postpone the call for a day or two," the doctor persisted. "You're sure you're fine. I think you're fine, but you're the President and we all have to know for sure you're fine."

"It's an important call," the President stressed, knowing he would have to give way.

"If it's important, then all the more reason to make sure you're in peak condition." The doctor knew that the Middle East was on the edge of a serious escalation of hostilities. "Important matters take time and energy. I'm here to make sure you've got both in abundance."

II.

When troubles come...

"COME in, Fred," said Cleveland. Cleveland didn't like Fred Tyler but he was a safe pair of hands. He could take crises in his stride.

Fred Tyler was a big man in his fifties, with a full head of thick grey hair. He was a man you couldn't ignore. He had a loud, booming voice which, when deployed in a contentious debate on the floor of the House, could silence the most recalcitrant and rumbustious opposition.

"Now tell me what is going on with the Israelis." Cleveland knew there was trouble brewing but Tyler had asked for an urgent meeting with him before the transatlantic call, so Cleveland deduced there were further developments. Yitzhak Sharon, the Israeli Prime

Minister, was a shrewd political operator and he might have decided that bold action was called for. What "bold" might mean was deeply worrying.

"We have a problem," said Fred. "The Israelis are going ahead with the new settlements."

"I thought they had postponed all new settlement plans, pending the corruption charges against Sharon."

"Yitzhak has declared a state of emergency. In the circumstances, the charges have been dropped," Fred explained.

"That's a pretty obvious, unsubtle ploy, isn't it?"

"No, not this time," said Fred. "It seems factions within Hamas have had enough, whether or not the new settlements go ahead. Iran is prepared to back them. There are plans to hit Israel hard, and I mean hard."

Cleveland gave a sigh of exasperation. "Well, it still sounds likely to me that Sharon has engineered a crisis to avoid corruption charges. In any case, I thought Haywood had told the Israelis to cool it."

"He has," Fred confirmed. "But they've told him they are going ahead anyway. Apparently, they told him that if he wants a second term as President, he had better get in line behind them."

"Really? And what did Robert say?"

"I don't know but I think you're about to find out this

afternoon," Fred replied.

"So are we in for another Intifada with a few thousand, mainly Palestinian, casualties?"

"It could be a lot worse than that," said Fred. "According to MI6, Iran is arming the Hamas faction with modern weapons. There's enough of them, if properly armed, to cause real problems. They are getting ready for a battle. As I said, there are rumours they will go ahead even if Israel doesn't annex more Palestinian land."

"I'm sure Israel can look after itself."

"Not necessarily," said Fred. "This time Hamas will have state-of-the-art weapons, supplied by China."

"Are you saying China is supplying Hamas with arms?"

"Yes. They're supplying arms to dealers in Lebanon who are then selling them to Iran who are supplying them to Hamas."

"What interest does China have in stirring up trouble for Israel? China and Israel have excellent diplomatic relations."

"You'll have to ask them," said Fred. "If you ask me, this is not about China's relations with Israel; it's about China's fractious relationship with the USA. They're fed up with Washington bad-mouthing them about human rights abuses, not to mention their political, industrial and commercial espionage, so they've decided to embroil the USA in a Middle East conflagration. With American help, Israel will probably win, but the rest of the world will be appalled at the cost in lives caused by Israel's illegal attempt, backed by the US, to annex other people's homes and land. And if by any chance Israel loses, the USA will be utterly humiliated, exposed as unable even to defend its protégé and key strategic ally in the Middle East. Either way, it will distract America and cost it money."

Cleveland leaned back in his chair to process what Fred had told him. He had been hoping that the Middle East situation was not an urgent priority. Evidently he was wrong. "What do you think Haywood wants from us?"

"Probably a shoulder to cry on," Fred replied with a laugh. "Israel is, for the US, a much loved, wayward child. The US tries to rein in Israel's excesses, but at the end of the day, it will do anything to protect its offspring. It has no choice."

"But all hell could break loose if someone doesn't do something."

"Absolutely right. And given that Haywood is the US President and you are the UK Prime Minister, I guess you're the guys in the hot seat. Great men do great things at such times."

Cleveland grunted. "Such as?"

"Well, Haywood could try to persuade Sharon to hold back on the settlements. That may not stop Hamas from launching its campaign, but if Israel goes ahead with the settlements, it's certain Hamas will strike."

"From what you've said, Sharon's not in listening mode."

"And we can work our way back through the weapons supply chain to try to persuade the governments of Lebanon, Iran and China that what they are doing will have incalculable and uncontrollable consequences."

"And do you think that'll work?" Cleveland asked. He had a high regard for Tyler's knowledge of the region and his judgement of such complex issues.

"No," said Tyler. "Probably not."

12.

Family matters

"SO, what am I supposed to do with you?" Archie Kildare asked. "Strictly speaking, I should have you arrested and charged. Let's put it this way, if I don't, Cleveland will probably have *me* arrested and charged. At the very least he'll fire me."

After Jess's homily in praise of miracles, Archie had spent time thinking and pondering his next move. "Strictly speaking, you haven't done any real or lasting damage," he continued. "Your crowd of fans dispersed in an orderly fashion, and although you buggered up our Comms and Security, you also kindly unbuggered it, assuming you were actually in some inexplicable way responsible for the problem and its solution."

"You are surprisingly irrational and confused for someone regarded as highly intelligent," Jess said in a tone that suggested sympathy as much as criticism. "Have you decided yet whether I am who I say I am? If I am *not* who I say I am, you can confidently treat me as an eccentric who has done little or no harm and probably requires sympathy and counselling. On the other hand, if you even half believe that I am who I say I am, if you entertain for an instant the notion that I did actually 'bugger' and 'unbugger' your Comms, and if you even half believe I am the Scion of God, your ruminations are utterly pointless. This afternoon will mark the beginning of a change in history as momentous as any that has gone before."

Kildare decided to humour her. She was right. He hadn't made up his mind about her. But he liked her company. Daughter of God or a misguided mystic, she was a compelling presence. "You said earlier that God was all for taking us out immediately but you have come to give us another chance. Is there some kind of rift between you and God?"

Jess hesitated. For the first time, she seemed almost unsure of herself. "This is not a matter I would normally discuss with others, but since the odds are that shortly you will be annihilated with the rest of your kind, what harm can come of it? I have never really seen eye to eye with God. Children rarely see eye to eye with their parents. You know that. After all, you were made in God's image."

"Woah!" exclaimed Archie. "I'm no religious scholar but surely the doctrine of the Trinity says you, God and the Holy Spirit are all one."

"Yes, but there would be no point in distinguishing three entities if we were all completely identical," Jess explained. "Let's face it, if you know the Old and the New Testament, you must have noticed there are some pretty conspicuous differences in attitude between God and what I taught. He chose a small tribe as his favourites, encouraged genocide so they could have a land of their own, destroyed whole cities – men, women and children – because he considered some of the inhabitants sinners, and regularly resorted to smiting anyone who disobeyed Him. He was so self-obsessed that he asked Abraham to sacrifice his son, just to prove how much he loved God. I, on the other hand, taught you to love your fellow men, to forgive those who do you wrong, to turn the other cheek. I spoke for tolerance and understanding. And I embraced the whole world – *all* the races of mankind, not just a small, randomly selected Semitic tribe. Yes, God and I have had, and still have, our differences."

"So, when you came last time, were you doing God's will or your own?" Archie was genuinely interested.

"An excellent question!" said Jess, "It is just possible I have underestimated you. The answer is both. I came to redeem mankind, but not by being crucified. I came to tell mankind how to behave. Crucifixion was never part of the plan. Come on! How would mankind's crucifixion of their Saviour redeem mankind? If eating a forbidden apple was enough to bring about the fall of man, nailing God's son to a cross was one weird form of redemption. What twisted logic could work that one out? Crucifying me simply reconfirmed the grip that all the flaws of human nature – hate, cruelty, lust for power, injustice – have their claws deep in the heart of man."

"But you say now that if we don't do what you want, you'll make us obey you. So have you changed your mind? Are you back on God's team, so to speak?"

"I see now that I was asking too much of you last time. My teachings made an impression, but they were subverted by the powerful – the rulers and the clerics. Constantine took the sign of the cross to augur his victory in battle against Maxentius. In an appalling distortion of my message, the sign of the Prince of Peace was conscripted into leading the cavalry charge that gave Constantine the keys of Rome. In the Middle Ages, the bloody crusades in which noble knights and their yeomen raped and murdered their way from the English Channel to Jerusalem, killing Christians and Muslims alike, were carried out in my name. In most wars between Christian states, both sides have claimed to be fighting with me on their side. Mine was a message of compassion and forgiveness, not vengeance and butchery. So no, I'm not back on God's team, but I'm not an idiot. I won't make the same mistake twice. This time, if I don't succeed, it's you, not me, that will be crucified."

Just as Jess finished delivering her sinister warning, the buzzer in Archie Kildare's office sounded.

"Yes?" Archie said into the intercom.

"My conference call with the US President has been cancelled," the PM said. "Come to my office, and bring that woman with you."

13.

Coincidentally

WHEN they reached Cleveland's outer office, Archie asked Jess to wait there while he had a quick word with Cleveland. Jess complied, settling into one of the armchairs and accepting Fiona's offer of refreshment.

Archie knocked and entered Cleveland's office.

"What's her background?" asked the PM without any preliminaries.

"Sorry, but I haven't made much progress on that front. For obvious reasons, she insists that there won't be any record of her after 33 AD. I've sent a sample of her DNA to the police lab to see if she's on any of our databases."

"Did she give a sample willingly?"

"No, she gave it unwittingly. I gave her a mug of tea and sent her mug to the lab. If there's anything to know we should have it in a couple of hours."

Cleveland appeared unsettled.

"Why was your conference call cancelled?" Archie prompted.

"Robert is unwell. He fainted. I'm assured it's not serious but they are running a few tests as a precaution."

"Quite a coincidence," Archie remarked.

Cleveland shook his head. "Yes," he conceded, "quite a coincidence – but that's all it is."

"We seem to be having rather a lot of coincidences," Archie suggested.

"Yes, we are. And you can add to them the cancellation of my trip to Brussels."

"Really?" Archie had been about to argue that one coincidence was of little or no significance; two related coincidences should raise an eyebrow; three was really puzzling, throwing the coincidence hypothesis into doubt. But four was surely too much for the hypothesis to survive. "Perhaps we are going to have to take Jess seriously," he hazarded.

"No," said Cleveland flatly. "No. We're not going to do that because that would be stupid."

"Funnily enough, that's precisely what Jess said I

was. But stupid or not, I think it's a bit perverse to put everything down to coincidence if the coincidences keep happening. The Brussels cancellation is number four."

"No," Cleveland repeated. "Brussels cancelled because the Council is deeply worried about the Middle East crisis and they have suggested, very sensibly, that it would be best to postpone my trip until I've spoken to Robert. So coincidence four is simply a direct consequence of coincidence three."

Archie shrugged. "I'm just saying that Jess said, right from the start, that she would see you, and although you said she wouldn't, she has. She said she would close down our Comms, and our Comms closed down. She said she would restart them, and they restarted. She said you should keep the rest of today clear. You said you couldn't. Yet here you are with the whole of the rest of the day at your disposal."

"She managed to see me because of the incompetence of Security and my own staff, including you," said Cleveland. "I admit the Comms going down and restarting was a coincidence, but as Security pointed out, it has happened before. As for Robert, he's been under a lot of pressure for some time. He's overweight, he's in his late sixties and he's got Sharon about to put a match to the entire Middle East. It's enough to make the fittest man faint."

"Fair enough," said Archie. "So why did you ask me to bring Jess along?"

"Because although I don't for one minute believe this Second Coming nonsense, I have a feeling we should know more about her before casting her into the dungeon. She might even be useful to us."

Archie was surprised. "She thinks it's the other way round."

"She raised a mob – sorry, she organised a march – which is interesting," Cleveland explained. "But much more interesting is that she controlled the mob she raised. They took no notice of the police. They ignored Juliet. But they obeyed her. An intelligent, focused, attractive, charismatic black woman who knows how to motivate and control people is just what every political party and every government needs today. In a way, she actually is a gift from heaven."

"Shall I bring this heavenly gift in from the outer office?" enquired Archie.

"Yes," said Cleveland. "Bring her in and then leave. I want to talk to her alone."

14.

Fit people don't faint

THE US Vice President and the President's wife both waited anxiously at the President's bedside in his room at the Bethesda Naval Hospital. His wife was simply concerned for her husband's health. Vice President Hank Allbright, too, was concerned about the health issue, but uppermost in his mind was the realisation that if the President was really ill – or even dying – *he* might actually become the President of the United States. Of course, he had known this to be a possibility upon his appointment, but on this bright, sunny morning, the reality of it struck him like a lightning bolt. Given the intimidating problems the country and the world faced, the prospect of taking over the Presidency filled Hank

Allbright with mixed emotions.

Robert Haywood, the US President, was in good spirits.

"I keep telling you, there's nothing wrong with me," he said.

"You fainted," his wife reminded him. "Fit people don't faint."

The Senior Consultant entered. "We've carried out every possible test and they all tell the same story. You're as fit as a fiddle. The only slight abnormality is marginally low blood pressure, a pulse rate at just below sixty at rest, but in a man of your age, that's a positive."

"So why did he faint?" his wife asked.

"Difficult to say. It could be postural hypotension. If you have low blood pressure and you stand up suddenly, you can feel dizzy and faint. It's possible but, as I say, all the vital organs are in excellent shape. Nothing wrong with your heart, Mr President. I suggest you take it easy for the next few days if you can. But there's no reason for you to stay in hospital or, indeed, have close medical supervision. By God, I wish I was as healthy as you."

The President thanked the Senior Consultant. "That's it," said Haywood. "Everyone out. I'll be dressed and ready to leave in ten minutes." There were general murmurs of relief as the room emptied. The President went through to the bathroom. He looked in the mirror. "Postural hypotension, huh? More likely 'Unexplained Incidence of Presidential Fainting Syndrome'."

15.

This time will be different

ARCHIE Kildare ushered Jess into the PM's office and left.

Cleveland invited Jess to sit in an armchair and he then sat in another one facing her. For a moment he said nothing. Then he spoke.

"You're a bit of a mystery," he began. "You don't seem to be delusional, but you can't really believe you are the Messiah."

"I don't believe I am the Messiah any more than you believe you are James Cleveland," Jess said lightly. "We are what we are."

Cleveland shook his head, not in a negative manner

but more as a means of shaking the various thoughts in his head into some form of order. He tried a different tack.

"All these coincidences – I must admit they are strange."

"What coincidences?" Jess asked. "There have been no coincidences. When there is a simple explanation for a chain of events, the sensible, rational man accepts the obvious explanation. Only a fool fumbles around in a world of superstition to explain events in some other way."

"And your simple, unsuperstitious explanation is that you are the Second Coming of Jesus?" There was more than a hint of mockery in his question.

"I know who I am. I know what I have done. You, on the other hand, are not so sure of who you are and even less sure of what you should do. As for your assessment of me, surely you can see that invoking coincidence to explain a series of foretold and clearly connected, predicted events is to retreat into a world of unreason and superstition."

Cleveland frowned. The conversation was not heading in the right direction. Again, he changed tack.

"Please try to see it from my point of view," he appealed. "If I accepted your claims, I would be relieved of office in short order. The men in white coats would take me away. In fact, they would take both of us away, and that wouldn't suit either of us."

"I understand your difficulty," Jess replied. "But you have to understand that what I am going to ask you to do is far more difficult. I am going to ask you to change the course of history. You really don't have time to worry about what others will think of you. You have to help me establish fair and free trade throughout the world, effect a fairer distribution of wealth, devise a means of stopping a war in the Middle East and come up with a way of persuading mankind to nurture not rape the planet. In this context, you must agree that your concerns about what others will think of you are pretty trivial."

Cleveland laughed. "I'm beginning to like you," he confided. "You have magnificent ambitions, all of which I thoroughly endorse. My problem is how to achieve such noble goals. I'm with you all the way. The problem is the other eight billion people."

"Not so," said Jess. "Most of the other eight billion also agree with me, not because they embrace high moral values but because they are oppressed and would like to live in a fairer world. The problem is you and your friends. The problem is the system of which you and your friends are the creators, the product and the sustainers."

"Oh dear," said Cleveland. "It's the same old story. It's all the fault of the rich and powerful. They are all greedy and corrupt. The problem with that analysis is that the system is the product of human nature. That's what human beings are like. Take any poor man and give him wealth and power and he will behave in exactly the same way as the rich and powerful. In fact, he may be even worse because he won't have any grasp of the limits most of the rich and powerful have learned to accept in order to ensure their survival."

"That's why I am here," said Jess. "I'm here to change human nature."

"And how do you think one black woman, however personable and charismatic you may be, can possibly change human nature?"

"This time is different," said Jess. "Last time, I tried to persuade mankind. I cured the sick. I raised the dead. I gave you the Sermon on the Mount. This time will be different."

"So no curing of the sick this time?" Cleveland couldn't help himself. He didn't believe in Jess, but when someone you love is ill, you will clutch at any straw. "My wife is being treated for cancer," he explained.

"Performing miracles to help individuals sent the wrong signal," Jess replied. "It distracted attention from my core message. This time I intend to use my powers to compel you to follow the right path. If you refuse, with regret I will destroy you."

Cleveland's eyes widened. He had tried to humour her, but now she had gone too far. She was a loose cannon, no good to party or government. Charismatic, certainly. Self-assured, undoubtedly. But delusional, unpredictable and dangerous. What a pity, he thought.

"May I ask you a question?" Jess's voice was soft, almost soothing, just as Archie Kildare had described it.

"Yes, of course."

"How's your headache?"

"Oh that," said Cleveland. "I'd forgotten about that. It's completely gone."

oooOooo

The phone rang.

"I've just been given the results on Jess's DNA," said Archie uncertainly.

Cleveland thought of asking Jess to leave but he hadn't finished with her, and since she couldn't hear what Archie was saying, there was no harm in letting her stay.

"Well?" Cleveland hoped that the results would give

them a lead to her identity. It would at least indicate her racial type and her possible geographical origin. Assuming it was normal, it would comprehensively undermine her claim to divine origin, although he realised she could claim that when she manifested in human form, obviously she had to incorporate human DNA.

"It's nothing," said Archie.

"Good news," said Cleveland assuming Archie was confirming his supposition of normality.

"No," said Archie. "When I say nothing, I mean nothing. They didn't find any DNA."

"That's a pity. You'll have to try again," said Cleveland.

"Right," said Archie. He wasn't going to argue, but he had already sent a second sample when the first returned a negative result, and the second sample had proved equally unforthcoming. Neither sample had provided any DNA for analysis.

16.

Who's the mad one?

THE door of Cleveland's office burst open and Fred Tyler came in.

"Sorry, but I've got some pretty bad news," said Tyler before he noticed Jess. "Oh, Fiona didn't say you had company."

"This is Jess," Cleveland said. "She led and then dispersed this morning's demo."

Fred frowned. He wanted to say *Get her out of here. This is for your ears only*, but he didn't. He expected Cleveland to tell the woman to go, but Cleveland didn't. Instead, Cleveland asked him what had happened. And Fred Tyler told him.

"The Israelis are planning a pre-emptive strike on

Hamas in the West Bank, on Hezbollah in Lebanon and on Tehran, with the intention of wiping out the Supreme leader, the Council of Guardians and most of the top clerics in the Iranian government."

"How do you know this?" Cleveland asked.

"I've got it on the best authority. I've no doubt the intel is good. It gets worse," Tyler continued. "Sharon plans to issue a warning to the Iranian government that if there is any retaliation – say the Revolutionary Guard tries to respond – he will not hesitate to use tactical nuclear weapons to deal with them."

"Is he mad?" Cleveland shrieked.

"According to my sources, he says he's going to put an end to the uncertainty that is destabilising the Middle East. He says it's time the Arabs accepted the reality that Israel is the most powerful nation in the region bar none, and that any nation that won't accept Israeli hegemony will face dire consequences."

"The Arabs will never accept that," said Cleveland. "Did he really use the word hegemony? Is he trying to provoke a war with every Arab state?"

"It seems he's learned that Haywood is ill. He thinks that the US and the UK have taken their eyes off the ball. He knows the EU will talk but do nothing. So he believes there will never be a better opportunity than now to settle all Israel's problems."

"How long have we got?" Cleveland asked.

"Four days," Tyler answered. "He plans to strike this Friday. Muslims will be at prayers, at the beginning of their weekend."

"What do you suggest we do?" Cleveland knew it would be his decision but he wanted Tyler's advice.

"I'll be honest," said Tyler. "There's not much we can do. Diplomatic representations are pointless. It's far too late for that. We could reveal Sharon's plans to the world, but that would be highly dangerous and contrary to every diplomatic convention. Through the US we are closely allied with Israel. We would be doing irreparable harm to Israel, not to mention our relations with the US. We could kiss goodbye to our intelligence participation in the Five Eyes."

"What about China?" Cleveland was exploring other possible implications. "How will they react if Israel annihilates the forces they've been arming? Are we looking at a world war?"

Jess interrupted: "Tell Sharon that if he attempts to launch such a campaign, he will die before he can give the order."

Both Cleveland and Tyler looked at her with astonishment. Tyler looked to Cleveland for some explanation.

"She believes she's Jesus and this is the Second Coming," Cleveland said waving a hand dismissively in her direction.

"What!" Tyler exploded. "For Christ's sake, get her out of here. The woman's obviously mad."

"I'm mad?" Jess laughed. "You two discuss an imminent Armageddon in the Middle East, a possibly nuclear conflagration that could involve the whole world and kill hundreds of millions of people. You conclude that there is nothing you can do – and I'm the mad one?"

"Making silly predictions and thinking they constitute a credible threat is beyond madness," said Tyler. He looked directly at Jess. He was surprised to note that she was entirely uncowed by his commanding presence and loud voice. He went on to the attack. "You are clearly a mentally challenged individual," he boomed. "You can't be Jesus, dear, because you are a woman. He was a man. Then again, you are black – of negroid origin. He was a Jew, presumably with an olive complexion. And you are alive, albeit insane, in the twenty-first century. He, assuming he ever existed, was put to death a couple of thousand years ago."

"Nevertheless, Sharon will die if he attempts to go ahead with his plan," Jess said undaunted.

Cleveland could see Fred Tyler was losing his temper. The Foreign Secretary really had no idea why the black woman was present, and he was even more disturbed that he had not immediately queried her presence and demanded her absence.

Cleveland addressed Jess: "I'd be grateful if you would wait in the outer office."

Jess moved towards the door. "Discuss and decide as you wish," she said as she opened it to leave, "but what I say, goes, and what I say will happen, will happen."

When she left, Fred Tyler expressed the view that the whole world was going mad. "Who the hell is that woman?" he asked. "You realise you can't let her go. She's clearly unhinged and now she knows about Israel's plans. Why was she in here anyway?"

"Why did you tell me what Sharon has in mind in front of her?" Cleveland countered.

"I assumed that as you didn't ask her to leave, I could tell you what was happening."

"No harm done," said Cleveland soothingly. "As you say, she seems entirely unhinged, in which case her threats against Sharon are harmless. If, on the other hand, Sharon dies – and she has an uncanny knack of making predictions that prove to be right – the problem could be solved – or at least postponed – without our intervention."

"Come on, James!" Tyler exclaimed. "You can't be taking this deluded woman seriously."

"Of course not," said Cleveland. "No, of course I don't believe her, but what does it matter? If she's wrong, we're in no worse plight than before. It seems to me our best course is masterly inaction. We'll form a working group to convene at Chequers tomorrow morning. Bring your best people. We need to analyse the situation before we do anything."

"Don't you mean 'instead of doing something'?" Tyler suggested, and then added: "And what about her?"

"We'll take her with us. We have to. As you say, she knows too much."

17.

Mossad in London

NO more than twenty minutes after the end of the conversation in Cleveland's office, the London-based Mossad unit was relaying a heavily encrypted message to their superiors in Jerusalem. The message was long because it reported the meeting in detail, in particular the presence and contribution of the woman Jess.

They had informed Jerusalem of the march on Downing Street that morning, simply as a matter of course. Any potential security issue was always logged and reported. They had even mentioned that the leader, a black woman, had been detained in 10 Downing Street. But at the time, they had not investigated Jess any further.

They knew from monitoring her conversations with

Cleveland and Kildare that she claimed to be the Messiah, paying mankind a second visit, but not surprisingly they had assumed she was insane and would be sectioned and removed. They saw it as an interesting and amusing but irrelevant breach of the UK's always flaky security.

Before sending the message they ran the little they knew about her through every database at their disposal but had found nothing. They were embarrassed. They knew they would receive an urgent request for full details about the woman who had threatened to kill the Israeli leader. They decided it was best to confess immediately that they had no information about the woman – only that she was black, probably Somali, and had green eyes – and she was the one who had organised the fairly large demonstration, purpose unknown, in Downing Street.

Despite their attempts to pre-empt criticism, questions came back thick and fast: Is she Arab? Does she have any connection with any Arab terrorist group? Does she have links with any Russian or Chinese officials? What is her sexual orientation? Is she in a sexual relationship with anyone? What is her background? Does she have a history of mental illness? What was the demonstration about? At the very least, what is her family name?

The head of the Mossad unit in London had no answers. Always acutely sensitive to his career prospects, he was wondering how this extraordinary episode would play out. In essence, he had reported that a mysterious woman had somehow inveigled her way into the British Prime Minister's office in London and been privy to a top-secret meeting in which the entirety of Israel's secret plans to remould the Middle East (code name Cyrus) had been openly discussed, during which the aforementioned woman said she would kill Yitzhak Sharon or have him killed before he could implement his plan. Even more strangely, the British Prime Minister and the Foreign Secretary had not immediately arrested the woman, nor had they informed Israel. Instead, they had said that if by any chance she succeeded, it would save them a great deal of trouble, a sentiment unlikely to be well received in Jerusalem. The head of Mossad in London wondered whether he would be promoted for his prompt action in reporting the bizarre event or would find his career blighted by his lack of foreknowledge and his inability to provide any useful information now.

"Kill her," was the blunt instruction.

Evidently, Mossad in Jerusalem had lost patience with the exchange of encrypted messages. By the time they issued their order, they had listened to the recording of the meeting in Cleveland's office. It was obvious she was part of an organisation capable of mobilising followers to do its bidding. They would immediately initiate their own global investigation to track down the organisation. In the meantime, best to eliminate the group's spokesperson. Her death would surely distract her fellow terrorists and disrupt their plans for a day or two.

Danny and Moshe were two of the most experienced field operatives in the whole of Mossad. They had both seen service in Lebanon. Daniel had successfully undertaken a number of assassinations in Europe; Moshe had worked in several north African countries.

Both took pride in their work. Most of the time, discretion was critical. The mark had to be killed in circumstances that were unsuspicious. The kill could be presented as an accident or as a suicide. Hit-and-run was Danny's favoured modus operandi. Moshe who had trained as a doctor and who still worked as a locum in Tel Aviv when not engaged on Mossad business, preferred the administration of heart-stopping drugs by unconventional means. But both were happy to adopt any of the many techniques in the Mossad manual for despatching enemies of Israel.

"There's no time to plan this one. We'll wait until she's out of the car at Chequers and put a bullet through her head," Danny said to Moshe as they climbed into their SUV. "We'll drive there now and set up."

Moshe drove. The car was a BMW M2. Danny sat in the back, checking their Barak (2000 HTR) sniper rifles.

"It's a tricky location," Moshe said. "I've picked a couple of spots to the south-east of the front of the building. I'm hoping we'll both have a good view. We'll do a recce in the night. We'll place some explosives to the south-west to go off when we shoot the woman. That'll distract the bodyguards and other security people and give us more time to disappear."

"What do you make of it all?" asked Danny. "The woman claims to be the Second Coming of Jesus. She's obviously mad but did you hear what the British Prime Minister said? H*er predictions have a habit of coming true*. She must have impressed him somehow. Otherwise he wouldn't have her in his office when they were discussing Operation Cyrus."

"Ours not to reason why," said Moshe. "But sure as hell she has to die."

They both chuckled.

18.

The path most travelled

"SO what's your plan?" Archie asked Jess. "I hear you've just threatened to off the Israeli Prime Minister. Must have come as a bit of a shock to James. He tends to favour the diplomatic route out of tricky situations. Mind you, I'm not criticising you. If Sharon really intends to plunge the Middle East, and quite possibly the whole world, into a final cataclysmic conflict, I wouldn't stand in your way if you did take him out. I am, however, curious about ways and means."

Once again Archie had been put in charge of Jess. He was considered best equipped to investigate her while keeping an eye on where she was and what she did, and she seemed happy to spend time in his company.

Jess said nothing.

"When I say I'm curious, I'm really asking a question," Archie prompted.

"You seem obsessed with means, with how things happen. I've told you, what I will, happens. What does it matter how? You just have to know that if Sharon tries to push ahead with Operation Cyrus, he will die."

"That's not really an 'if'," said Archie. "Not if you know Sharon. He's not going to be put off by an implausible threat, nor by a real one for that matter."

"I haven't issued a threat – nor have I said I will kill him. I've said he will die. That is a statement of fact. It is true that I am the agency that will cause him to die, in the sense that I will it to be so, but I certainly don't need to involve myself in the mechanics of it."

All Archie said was "Right", but he thought she really was quite something, this black, probably Somali, woman with luminescent green eyes, fine features, a fine body, an intelligent if odd mind, an imperious manner and, quite possibly, one or two superpowers.

"You asked me to tell you my plan," Jess continued. "I will tell you because you have a part to play. First, I must stop the war that Sharon is planning. I cannot fulfil my objectives if the world is in turmoil. I have a limited time to put humanity on a better path. If your time runs out, you and your planet will be blown away in an instant."

"Yes, you mentioned something like that before," Archie said. "No disrespect, but given that Man seems rather attached to the path he's on, what do you reckon are your odds of success? I mean we've been what we are throughout recorded history. There's likely to be some resistance to change."

"How would you describe your path?" Jess asked.

Archie paused for thought. "Well, it's a mixed picture. We've done very well in some respects and I'm afraid rather badly in others."

"I think you're being rather generous to your kind. I would say your main distinguishing features are that you are a greedy, selfish, often cruel, self-obsessed bunch of hypocrites. You blather on about justice and equality of opportunity and then complain if your government gives 0.7% of your GDP in aid to poverty-stricken nations where children die of starvation. That's not even a penny in the pound.

"And then there's your idiotic self-obsession. Take your social media. What on earth gave any of you the idea that your uniformly tedious, humdrum lives could be of any possible interest to anyone other than yourselves? Yet these online community websites are immensely successful. Why? Because you're all equally deluded.

"Then there's all that gender nonsense. God is convinced you've completely lost the plot. When he created you and your world, he took immense care to ensure there were some basic certainties that would help you to discern order in an intimidating and, in other respects, seemingly anarchic world. So he made the survival of the species dependent on the binary nature of sex. Simple, straightforward, incontrovertible. But no, someone felt the need to come up with the notion of gender as a separate entity which could be out of kilter with sex. He admires ingenuity but he's taken this particular eccentricity as a personal insult."

"Hold on!" Archie said, interrupting what seemed likely to be a very long diatribe against mankind. "Last time you were here I thought you said that God cared about everything, even the death of a sparrow, and especially about us, even to the extent of counting the number of hairs on our head."

"I was exaggerating," said Jess.

"Well, if you feel like that," said Archie, amazed and amused that he was taking Jess so seriously, "why have you bothered to come back? Why are you trying to save us?"

"It's complicated," Jess said with a sigh.

"Try me," said Archie. "It may surprise you to know

that I'm pretty familiar with the New Testament and I'm really curious. Why has the man who said 'turn the other cheek' come back as a woman who is now happily planning the assassination of an eminent politician? Change of heart?"

"If you know the New Testament, you will know that this time I am bringing with me all the power of the Creator and that I am here to judge you."

Archie grunted. "Well, that doesn't sound too complicated – unpleasant, unfair, cruel perhaps, but not complicated."

"It's complicated because I want to save you," said Jess simply.

"So things haven't changed," said Archie. "You still want to save us. But I thought you said God was fed up with us and was all for calling it a day – Judgement Day, I guess."

"You're not very good at listening. I've explained that God and I have our differences, irreconcilable differences. God has his good points. He loves creating and He's very good at it. Give Him nothing and He'll make something. Give Him less and He'll make more. And He put that gift of creativity into mankind. But as to what happens after He's exercised his creativity, He's really not on it."

"Isn't that so we can exercise free will?" Archie was determined to probe Jess's mind. If she was a fake, surely she wouldn't present herself as alienated from God. That would immediately raise doubts about her authenticity. In a weird way, the fact that she insisted that she and God didn't see eye to eye gave some credibility to her story.

"Yes, He gave you freewill. But He also gave you diseases and natural disasters, which have nothing to do with free will and everything to do with Him failing to take care of, and responsibility for, what He's created. And when things go wrong, He has a tendency to say it's got nothing to do with Him. He blames everyone but Himself and then quite often punishes those He's blamed. Take my crucifixion. How did that happen? The Romans who had all the power wanted to let me go. But no, a bunch of Pharisees intervened and I end up nailed to a tree. And I'm His only child."

"You're very critical of your Father." Archie, although not at all religious, was genuinely shocked. "You do realise that if what you're saying were true, you'd be overthrowing the whole of Christian theology."

"As far as I can see, there's not much to overthrow in the West," said Jess. "Most of you are atheists or at best agnostics."

"You're forgetting about Middle America and the

evangelical movement in many countries. In any case, if you take the world as a whole, the majority still believe in God or gods."

"That's another bone of contention between me and Him," said Jess bitterly. "His obsession with faith! What's that all about? First, He hides Himself. Then he makes it a condition of His approval that you believe in Him, an entirely invisible entity."

"And you don't?" Archie queried. "You don't demand belief in you?"

"No, of course not," snapped Jess. "First, I don't ask anyone to believe in me, merely to take my advice on how to conduct themselves. Secondly, when I issue my advice, I come in person and deliver it to mankind, face to face, so to speak."

"And what gives you the right to tell us how to behave?" Archie asked. "I mean it's obvious you're acting without God's full approval."

"You are God's greatest creation," Jess replied solemnly. "I'm not prepared to write you off yet, even if He is. I want you to fulfil your destiny. You have almost incomprehensible potential. But you also have flaws, weaknesses – and in some ways you are incredibly stupid. If I don't intervene, you will have wrecked the planet in a couple of hundred years. All Earth's resources will dwindle. In the ensuing wars for survival, you will paradoxically ensure Man is completely annihilated."

"Sounds as though we're hardly worth saving," hazarded Archie.

Suddenly Jess lost interest in the conversation. "I have a small matter to attend to. I'm sure we can continue our little chat at another time."

Archie laughed. "Fair enough, but I'm not going anywhere and neither are you."

"That's fine," Jess said unperturbed. "I just need you to shut up."

19.

Somalis don't have green eyes

DANNY and Moshe were making good progress. Traffic was light; the rush hour was long past. They sped along the A413, then turned left onto Dunsmore Lane and drove straight on through the forest to Lodge Hill.

At the same time, some way ahead of the assassins, Sid Allaway was driving his HGV along Missenden Road towards Chequers. He had been despatched to deliver a special consignment of security equipment (cameras, lights, sensors and computers) to Chequers, to bolster security as part of the preparations for the large party arriving from London the following day. He couldn't understand why they left these things until the last minute; they were going to have to work all night to install even half of the consignment. It was no skin off his nose – he earned double for these urgent deliveries.

Danny opened the central console, took out a boiled sweet and removed the plastic wrapping with his teeth before popping the humbug in his mouth. "You know there's a funny side to all this," he said, the sweet bulging in one of his cheeks.

"Really?" said Moshe. "Nothing particularly funny about taking out a terrorist."

"Not usually," Danny continued. "But this one claims to be the Messiah on a return visit. And we've been instructed to take her out. Don't you see? We're doing it again."

Moshe was not particularly amused. "Doing what again?"

"We're killing the Messiah, like we did last time."

Moshe shook his head. He liked Danny but sometimes he could be incredibly irritating.

Sid Allaway considered turning on his radio. He could tune it to Radio 2. It would take him about ten minutes to reach Chequers, half an hour to unload, and then an hour back to London. It had started to rain. That would slow him down so it might take more than an hour. He would catch the news now and be ready for some easy listening on the way back.

Moshe took out a sweet too. "She's not the Messiah," he explained to Danny as he unwrapped it. "She's a black Somali woman who's the leader of an as yet unidentified terrorist organisation, hell-bent on assassinating our Prime Minister."

"So you say," said Danny, "but that's not the way others may see it. 'Jews shoot innocent civilian who claims to be Jesus'. How about that for a headline? Or 'Why have the Jews got it in for Jesus?' Or 'Will the Jews never learn?'"

Moshe turned left into Missenden Road. "That's not funny," he said, turning towards Danny.

Just as Sid Allaway was switching on the radio, a small animal ran across the road in front of him. "Bugger!" he said, braking hard in the middle of the narrow road. Instantly all his lights failed. They'd failed before. Apparently the fuse blew if you had your headlights on, your windscreen wipers on and your radio on all at the same time – and you braked. The garage had said it was a design fault.

Moshe turned into Missenden Road and put his foot down. The sooner they arrived and started the recce, the sooner he could stop Danny from droning on about a Messiah. He seemed obsessed with the notion that she claimed to be the Second Coming. "I tell you something," Danny said. "She can't be Somalian. Somalis don't have green eyes."

The assassins' car ran into the back of the unlit stationary HGV at about fifty-five miles an hour. Their seat belts would have saved them, but the car slid under the back of Sid's vehicle. Moshe was decapitated. Danny was seriously injured and had a chance of surviving, but then the car burst into flames. Sid was shaken but unhurt. He could do nothing to help Danny who was inextricably trapped under the floor of the HGV trailer.

20.

Stupid tenants

Tuesday

THE following morning the motorcade set out from London to Chequers. A car with four armed policemen led the way, followed by the Prime Minister's bulletproof car, with James Cleveland and Archie Kildare on board. Behind them were four more cars carrying Fred Tyler, Foreign Secretary, Andrew Purdy, Home Secretary, and an assortment of civil servants and advisers. Six police motorcyclists accompanied the convoy. Jess had been allocated a seat in Fred Tyler's car. He had suggested that she should travel with him so he could "take her measure", as he put it.

"It seems there was an accident last night," said Archie Kildare to James Cleveland in the prime-ministerial car. "We might be held up briefly. A car went into the back of a lorry on Missenden Road."

"Were they heading for Chequers?" Cleveland asked.

"The HGV was," Archie replied, listening intently to the newsfeed coming to him through an earpiece. "It was taking some technical equipment to Chequers to beef up security for us during our stay. As for the car, the police don't yet know. They're trying to identify the occupants now. It's difficult. They were both killed. The car burst into flames. As far as the police can tell, neither of the men was carrying any form of identification."

"Really! That's odd," Cleveland observed.

oooOooo

In the car behind, Fred Tyler had initiated a conversation with Jess. "So you're Jesus, are you?" he began. It was in his nature to take things head-on, not an obviously positive attribute for a Foreign Secretary.

"And you are the Foreign Secretary of the United Kingdom," said Jess.

"No one can doubt that I'm Foreign Secretary," said Fred, realising that the black Messiah in his car was nobody's fool. "However, there are those who might be just a little sceptical about your claimed provenance."

"I have not come to prove my identity," said Jess. "I am here to persuade the leaders of this world – and, indeed, men such as you – to mend your ways, to take your responsibilities seriously and to give mankind a chance to survive."

Tyler began to understand why Cleveland had been impressed. Of course she wasn't Jesus. But she had a calm authority about her not commonly associated with the delusional or the mentally challenged. He decided to take a more conciliatory approach. "I assume you are concerned about climate change and the threat to the planet's ecosystem. As are we. We recognise that if we fail to cut carbon emissions drastically, the global economy will be in danger of collapse within a couple of hundred years – perhaps even sooner."

"You have one week – or to be precise, five days," Jess said flatly.

Tyler laughed. "Aren't you being a little over-dramatic?"

"Had I not interceded on your behalf, you would be gone already," said Jess.

"How so?"

"It is God's opinion that you have failed," said Jess.

"How can I explain this to you? Assume you have designed the finest, most comfortable, most energy-efficient house, with a beautifully designed and perfectly tended garden. And assume you have let it to some seemingly intelligent, sensible and appreciative tenants. How would you feel if those tenants proved to be stupid, destructive and not in the least grateful? If they ruined the garden, trashed the house and squandered energy? You would feel disappointed, you would feel angry and you'd wish to throw them out. Am I right?"

Tyler nodded.

"Well, that's God's position," said Jess. "He wanted to blow you away immediately. On Sunday."

"And you stopped Him?" Tyler decided to go along with Jess's narrative.

"I presented a case to Him. I asked Him to give you one more chance, a chance you had been promised – my Second Coming."

"I see," said Tyler. "And you think one unknown black woman is going to persuade the powers that be that they should change their ways. And you think you can achieve this utterly impossible feat in a few days. Would you not agree you are being just a tad over-ambitious?"

"The last time I came, I managed to establish a religion that has dominated much of the world for two thousand years," said Jess. "Then I came as a man with olive skin, of a tribe under Roman rule, a tribe widely seen then as a nuisance by the civilised world. Today, as a black woman of African provenance, admittedly a continent in disarray, I am no more disadvantaged. Perhaps, less."

"Surely you see …" Fred began, intending to disabuse her of any hope of success.

"But this time," Jess interrupted, "I have the power to do as I think best. This time there is no Sanhedrin to falsely accuse me. There is no Roman governor, prefect of Judaea, to order my crucifixion. This time, I am the power. And if need be, I will exercise it."

oooOooo

"They were Mossad operatives," Archie exclaimed. He had just received confirmation of the two dead men in the car.

"What were they doing heading for Chequers?" Cleveland asked, alarmed.

"We don't know and the Israelis won't tell us," Archie replied. "Mossad's only admitted it was their people because they want the car and the bodies back. But we do know the dead men were on a mission to kill someone. The police found evidence of two sniper rifles and a small arsenal of weapons in the wreckage."

"But who?" Cleveland asked.

"Probably you – or Fred, because you didn't tell them about Jess and her plan to knock off the Israeli PM," Archie suggested. "Or Jess herself."

"But that would mean they knew about Jess," said Cleveland shocked.

"And they knew we were all setting out for Chequers this morning, and they knew it as soon as you decided we should go," Archie pointed out.

"Obviously, Security in Downing Street is as leaky as an Emmental bucket," said Cleveland ruefully.

21.

Chequers

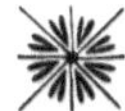

AFTER a brief delay at the scene of the previous night's accident, the motorcade arrived safely at Chequers.

Cleveland was keen to move things forward. "As soon as everyone has settled in, I want a meeting with Fred in the cabinet room."

His meetings with Jess the day before had unsettled him. From the moment she arrived, he'd had nothing but bad news. His control of affairs seemed to be slipping away. The Middle East crisis was clearly heading towards a catastrophic outcome. Even if Sharon could be persuaded to hold back, which was most unlikely, the Palestinians, who were bitter and frustrated, might still go ahead with a wave of terrorist attacks that would legitimise whatever punitive action Israel might decide to take.

What's more, his policy of masterly inaction had come apart. The Israelis must have been listening in to his meeting yesterday with Jess and Fred. They wouldn't be best pleased with his decision to say and do nothing. He could hear Sharon saying that such deceit was not the behaviour of a friendly nation – to which he would be sorely tempted to reply that sending a hit squad to eliminate someone at Chequers was at least as hostile.

The Israelis must also be wondering what kind of prime minister would discuss international affairs of such sensitivity in front of an unknown agitator. Indeed, Cleveland himself was pondering the same question. He decided to have Jess sent back to London under police escort to have her charged with some minor offence and heavily fined or briefly imprisoned. He didn't care which, so long as she was no longer around to unsettle him.

The only good news was that the threatened pandemic seemed to have been avoided. Following the fiasco in 2020, the WHO had surprisingly acted with exemplary speed and efficiency. The two hot spots, one in China and one in Vietnam, had been contained and to date, no other country had reported any cases.

Cleveland was the first to arrive in the cabinet room.

He had brought Fiona with him. He had scarcely settled into a chair when Fred Tyler burst in. "There's a popular uprising in Iran. Hundreds of thousands are on the streets. The Revolutionary Guard has been deployed. It looks serious."

"Are they calling for war against Israel?" Cleveland asked, fearful that the Iranian government had organised the demonstration to show popular support for the upcoming conflict with their Zionist enemy.

"No, they're demonstrating against their government," Fred replied. "They're fed up with the corruption of the clerics who run the show."

"Really?" Cleveland was stunned. "Where has this come from? I can't recall you mentioning a particularly high level of popular discontent in Iran. I know the people consider their government incompetent and corrupt, but I thought the clerics had a firm grip on power."

"So did I," said Fred. "I'm sorry but I can't explain it. There was no forewarning. It seems to be a spontaneous uprising."

"I need to talk to Haywood," Cleveland said to Fiona. "We need to know what the US is doing. If Haywood's not well enough to talk, get the Vice President. He'll be better than nothing."

"That's a close call," said Fred. "I don't think

Haywood knows what to do. The Vice President certainly won't. He's a total waste of space. He'd be out of his depth in a footbath. You need to talk to Sharon."

"Sharon won't take much notice of me if I don't have Haywood's backing," Cleveland replied. He didn't dispute Tyler's assessment of the American Vice President. "Knowing Sharon, he won't take any notice even if I do." Cleveland paused and then added, "I think you should contact your opposite number in Jerusalem and tell him to tell Sharon we strongly advise Israel to abandon Operation Cyrus. Given they're going to ignore our advice, it will be less humiliating for us if the advice has come from you rather than me."

"Less humiliating for you, not me," Tyler retorted. "In any case, I'm not sure I follow your reasoning. If you know our advice will be ignored, why give it? And why assume it will be ignored? Israel will know there is chaos in Tehran and several other cities. Surely Israel will want to see what happens in Tehran before launching all-out war on Iran's proxies? And if Hamas, Hezbollah and others can no longer be confident of Tehran's support, they might also like to take time to think twice."

"It's just as likely Israel will take chaos in Iran as the perfect opportunity to wipe out all its enemies," Cleveland replied. "You know Sharon."

"He's ruthless but he's not stupid," Tyler persisted. "I don't think he will initiate Operation Cyrus without at least the tacit approval of the US.

"We'll see," said Cleveland. "In the meantime, pass on our advice for restraint, and put our advice as strongly as you like."

22.

What is to be done?

AS he had not been invited to the PM's meeting, Archie Kildare sought out Jess. He had some news and some questions for her. She was under guard in one of the many guest rooms. Archie dismissed the guards, assuring them that Jess would do no harm. The guards left the room but remained stationed outside in the corridor.

With the guards dismissed, he turned his attention to Jess who seemed to be meditating. She was standing by the window, looking out at the courtyard and the lawns. Archie noted once again her beauty, her elegance and her authority. It was her authority that impressed him most. She seemed to exude self-confidence, not in a crude or strident way but as an unquestionable, irresistible force. She'd make a bloody good saleswoman, he thought.

"It goes from bad to worse," he started. "Iran is on the brink of revolution or a civil war."

She tore herself away from the window and turned her luminescent green eyes on him. He felt a shiver ripple through his whole body.

"And Israel is on the brink of initiating a Third World War," she replied in her soft, low voice. "What a mess!"

"I was rather hoping you had a plan to sort things out," said Archie. Of course it was a stupid remark. It implied she might have an answer, which was ridiculous. "I thought you said Sharon would be dead before he could initiate a strike." He reminded her of her words at the meeting with Cleveland and Tyler the previous day, words that had spread through No. 10 like wildfire.

"And so it shall be," said Jess. "I take no pleasure in ending Sharon's life but my regret is ameliorated by the knowledge that he had ordered my execution."

"How do you know he ordered your execution?" Archie asked. "Do you think you are in danger?"

Jess laughed. "Your head is full of conflicting thoughts and emotions. Am I who I say I am, or am I utterly deluded? Do I mean what I say, or am I an outrageous fantasist? When I foretell the future and I am proved right, am I the agency of events or just a lucky or well-informed guesser? The only certainty you have is that you find me" – she paused as she selected the correct word – "fascinating."

Archie was disconcerted and embarrassed.

Jess continued: "I can set your mind at rest on the Middle East crisis, at least for now. Look at your watch."

It took Archie a few seconds to realise she had given him an instruction. "It's 9.45," he said.

"Good," said Jess, "because Sharon is now dead, as is the Ayatollah, Muhammed Abbas. They have both succumbed to the new virus that threatens the world with a pandemic. You will think it an odd coincidence that they have both succumbed to the same ailment but it is less surprising when you discover that Sharon and Abbas recently attended a secret meeting in China at which China, assuming the mantle of the USA, attempted to initiate a Middle East peace process, unsuccessfully of course."

"How can you know all this?" Archie asked.

"Why do you doubt me?" Jess asked. "I've never understood it. You people have this ill-founded faith in common sense. Then when I perform a miracle, when I raise someone from the dead, when I raise myself from the dead, thus proving what I say is true, you still don't believe me and grimly hang on to your often ill-founded common sense."

"If Sharon and Abbas are dead, how come I haven't heard about it?" Archie asked defensively.

"Abbas died ten days ago," Jess replied. "The clerics tried to keep it quiet but news has now leaked out. The uprising was triggered by the rumour of his death. Many Iranians are hoping this is an opportunity for change. Sharon has only just died. The Israeli Government has been thrown into turmoil. Sharon's fractious coalition will fall apart. There will be no Operation Cyrus this side of the inevitable Israeli election. So, as I said, on that score you need not worry."

Archie said nothing. He was trying to digest what Jess had told him. She had made a couple of predictions that he would be able to verify or disprove. If her predictions were correct, he would have to conclude that either she genuinely had some superpower or she had an intelligence and black ops network at her disposal that put both Mossad and the SAS to shame.

The absurdity of the situation was not lost on him. He was sitting in a room with a beautiful black woman who purported to be Jesus and who, so far, had not put a foot wrong in maintaining her story. On the other hand, she had done nothing to prove conclusively that what she claimed was true. There had been one or two troubling coincidences but no proof.

And what was her mission? She claimed she had come to give Man one last chance, to put humanity on a better path. A grand ambition indeed, and a worthy – no essential – goal! But how, on God's good earth, could she hope to achieve it?

"You are wondering what I plan to do," said Jess. "It's simple. I should have tried it last time. I'm going to recalibrate the empathic function in human psychology, at least in the political leadership around the world. Last time I instructed everyone to love their neighbour as they loved themselves. There was a flaw in that exhortation, quite apart from its failure to gain traction in the hearts of most people. But no matter. This time I'm going to install in the minds of all world leaders a compulsion to feel themselves as their neighbours feel. In other words, they themselves will feel any pain they cause, or try to cause, others. Until politicians become used to this upgraded empathic faculty, some, I fear, will die. The pain and the burden of guilt they'll have to bear for starting wars, for permitting poverty, for complacently accepting starvation, for despoiling the planet will be so overwhelming that they'll find it intolerable. But as soon as they discover that they always feel the full extent of the pain they cause or intend to cause, they will radically alter their behaviour."

"They themselves will feel the pain they cause others?" Archie felt the need to make sure he understood. "You can do that?"

Suddenly Archie felt a wave of euphoria. He was in the presence of a supremely good person who was going to solve all the world's problems. There was no need for the idiotic bureaucratic processes that ground on with a life of their own while completely ignoring the reason for their existence. No more interminable meetings where the outcome, after months or years of negotiations, was as insubstantial as the mark left on the air by the billions of futile words exchanged. No more hypocrisy, because the price would be too high to pay. "This is so wonderful!" Archie shouted. He was excited beyond belief. "Wonderful! Wonderful! wonderful!"

As he emitted the last "wonderful", the feeling of euphoria abated and then disappeared altogether.

"I hope that answers your question," said Jess.

Once again, Archie fell silent. He was wondering whether his euphoria had been a spontaneous reaction to a brilliant strategy to bring sanity to the world, or whether Jess had inspired his feeling of euphoria simply to demonstrate her ability to control another's feelings.

After a few minutes he spoke: "What did you mean by saying there was a flaw in your instruction that 'we should love our neighbour as ourselves'?"

"Merely that most people don't love themselves," Jess responded immediately. "You're self-centred and selfish, but you don't love yourselves. Sadly, few of you are capable of real love. Most of what you call love is based on your own needs or wants. And on those rare occasions when any of you actually look into your own hearts, there's an awful lot of what you see there that you don't like, much less love."

"That's a little harsh." Although he knew he really wasn't up to it, Archie felt the need to defend humanity.

"Now answer me a question," Jess said, ignoring his feeble response. "When you are with me, you experience a mixture of thoughts and emotions – actually more a maelstrom – such that it is difficult to disentangle and codify. But I have noticed a strand that runs though your consciousness. You find me attractive. If you were responding to my persona, to my charisma, to my power, this would be unremarkable. But I discern a carnal component. Do you acknowledge this is so?"

Archie was completely flummoxed. "Absolutely not," he replied. Even if she were merely a delusional woman, any response to her of a sexual nature, given she was effectively under arrest, would have been entirely unacceptable. But if she were truly the Scion of God, present on Earth to fulfil the prophecy of the Second Coming, it would be beyond inappropriate. It would be blasphemous, disgraceful, hubristic, perverse, shameful ... Archie found himself compiling a thesaurus of sins and misdemeanours of which he felt himself guilty.

"Don't omit dishonesty and hypocrisy," said Jess helpfully, with a smile.

23.

Hate/love relations

WHEN his meeting with Tyler had ended, Cleveland stayed in the cabinet room, waiting for Fiona to put him through to Hank Allbright, the American Vice President.

"I'm told he's not available," Fiona told Cleveland.

"Not available!" Cleveland exploded. "Tell him to make himself available."

"It's rather early in Washington," Fiona objected tentatively.

"The Middle East is about to blow up in our faces and neither the President nor the Vice President is available. Tell them to get real and get their act together."

After two more attempts, Fiona succeeded in getting

Hank Allbright on the phone. The conversation did not get off to the best of starts.

"What the hell do you want?" shouted Hank. "It had better be good if it can't wait until office hours."

Cleveland felt anger welling up inside him, just like molten lava rising before breaking the surface of Yellowstone National Park and annihilating most of Middle America. He composed himself. "Good to talk to you too, Hank."

"Well?" was the abrupt, monosyllabic reply.

"I apologise for waking you at this time, but given we're on the verge of a war likely to consume the entire Middle East and possibly trigger a Third World War, I thought you might like to be kept in the loop. I seem to recall you're the Vice President."

"The Middle East is always on the verge of something or other," replied Hank sneeringly, but his voice now betrayed two emotions: regret for his ill-manners and panic in that he was not entirely sure where the Middle East was.

"Sharon is thinking of launching Operation Cyrus, and Iran is in the throes of an uprising," Cleveland summarised.

"What exactly is Operation Cyrus?" Hank asked. "And I thought we had Iraq sorted."

Cleveland switched the phone to mute. He turned to Fiona who was, as usual, listening in to the PM's important international calls. "The man's as thick as pig shit," said Cleveland. "They have three hundred and fifty million people to choose from and they come up with this."

Cleveland turned his speaker back on. "Is Robert available?" he asked.

"The President is feeling below par," Hank said, "and if he wasn't, he'd be in bed. So I guess either way, he's in bed, which is where I would be if I wasn't answering your call."

"Is there any point in me asking you where America stands on Sharon's plans to kick off World War Three?" Cleveland asked.

"I don't have to take this," said Hank, slamming down the phone. "If that fuck phones again, put him on hold and leave him there," he instructed his PA.

"As soon as it's 8.00 am in Washington, get hold of Haywood," Cleveland instructed Fiona. "Even if he's dying," he added, "or, given who would take over, especially if he's dying."

oooOooo

Following his abortive transatlantic call, Cleveland ordered a double espresso and a doughnut. He took the opportunity to phone his wife, Emma. She was back home after undergoing the first session of the second round of chemo.

"How are you, love?" he asked.

"I'm good," she replied.

"I know that," he said, with a laugh. "You're more than good. You're the best."

"I'm just a bit tired," said Emma. "Where are you?"

"I'm at Chequers. We have a bit of a crisis on our hands."

"You mean the Middle East," said Emma. "You're well worth your master's in euphemism."

"Thanks," said Cleveland. "You don't miss much."

"I don't think anyone could miss the rumours about Sharon and his dwindling supply of patience with the Palestinians."

"You'd be surprised," said Cleveland. "I just had a very brief chat with Hank Allbright and apart from confusing Iraq with Iran, which is a bit of a Presidential tradition, he didn't seem at all concerned or even aware."

"You shouldn't be too hard on him," said Emma. "Robert took him on as his running mate for the support he brought from Middle America. Hank's very popular along the Bible Belt. He doesn't have a passport and he's never been abroad. International affairs are not his strong suit. In any case, why are you talking to him? Is there something wrong with Robert?"

"Yes, he had a fainting fit a couple of days ago. I tried to set up a conference call with him but he was indisposed. His doctors say he's fine. They couldn't find anything wrong with him, but he's been told to rest."

"So that's why you were talking to Hank?" said Emma.

"Yes, but it was a mistake. In future if I have a choice, I'll talk to Robert rather than Hank, even if Robert's dead. I'm pretty sure I'd get more sense out of him."

Emma laughed.

"I miss you," said Cleveland.

"And I miss you too, but you've got bigger things to worry about than me. I'm fine. You just concentrate on preventing a Third World War."

24.

Difficulties overcome

AFTER his call to Emma, he was joined by Jess in his office. She was accompanied by Archie Kildare who was still supervising her.

"I've come to tell you what you must now do," said Jess, sitting down on a chair across from Cleveland's desk. "Please listen carefully. Time is of the essence."

"Excuse me," Cleveland interrupted. "I don't know how you keep walking in on me like this. Archie was supposed to be taking care of you. But I really must explain something to you. You are here under sufferance, simply because you know too much to be let out of our sight. You have no role here as an adviser. Indeed, you have no role here at all."

He had more to say but inexplicably he found he was unable to continue.

"Don't interrupt me again," Jess continued, her green eyes transfixing him. "I'm here to help. You must listen and then do as I say. The world – your world – is facing catastrophe. You – and by *you* I mean the leaders of the world – face problems that clearly you are ill-equipped to handle. The problems are great and it is questionable whether any of you have the intellectual capacity to deal with them. But far more importantly, human nature itself is defective." Jess paused, waiting for her last point to sink in.

"May I speak?" Cleveland hazarded.

Jess nodded.

"You are obviously a phenomenon but you're in a world of your own. You really can't tell me, a Prime Minister, what to do. We're a democracy. I was elected. No one voted for you."

"I am part of the Trinity that created the world," Jess replied. "The Creator does not need the votes of His creation. What He has created, He can destroy. I have explained to Archie that as far as God is concerned, you are at the end of the line. I have interceded on your behalf and, reluctantly, God has granted a small window for me to try to redeem you. I know it's a lot to take in, but you need to pick up. I'm on a tight schedule."

"You're on a tight schedule! So are we. We've got the risk of a Third World War and Armageddon to avert."

"Good," Jess responded. "We're on the same page. The only difference is, I can make things better and you can't."

"And assuming for a moment that I believe you," Cleveland said, "what's your plan?"

"Before I tell you my plan, I'm going to prove to you that I am the Second Coming," Jess said. "I don't have time for a grand gesture but take a piece of paper and write down ten digits at random."

Cleveland frowned but did as Jess asked. "I can't see what this will prove."

"You are a rational man. What are the chances of me guessing the first digit?"

"One in ten, obviously."

"What about the first and second digits?"

"One in a hundred."

"Very well." Jess took a piece of paper and wrote down ten digits. "Please compare."

All ten digits were correct and in the same order. "The odds against that happening by chance are trillions to one against. Does that satisfy you?"

"Not really," said Cleveland. "I'm impressed, but it's

just a magician's trick."

"I don't do tricks," said Jess. "How about this then?"

Cleveland gasped and then doubled up in pain. He felt as though he had been stabbed in the stomach and that his assailant was stirring and chopping his intestines with the knife.

"Enough!" he gasped. "Stop."

"Now perhaps you will do as I say," Jess said.

oooOooo

Of course there had been problems. In France, the President had been persuaded to comply, but members of his staff had proved resistant until they experienced the same painful coercion to which Cleveland himself had been subjected. It was as though everyone had an on/off pain switch. Do what the British Prime Minister asked of them or face the excruciating consequences.

In China, a senior minister had decided to kill the Paramount Leader to prevent his country from obeying what he saw as the demand of a former colonial power. It had been necessary to reduce the recalcitrant minister and all members of the Standing Committee of the National People's Congress to whimpering wrecks before they understood that not even the Chinese Communist Party could stand against the will of the enigmatic black woman who, it was now known, exercised extraordinary powers over the British Prime Minister and anyone else who stood in her way.

In Italy, there were unforeseen complications. When Cleveland phoned the Italian Prime Minister, Luigi Ferrari, he was swiftly persuaded to comply and accept the invitation to the G20 meeting. But the Italians had heard the absurd rumour that the enigmatic black woman, who was thought to be one of Cleveland's very close advisers, was claiming to be Jesus and Ferrari thought it only polite to inform the Vatican. The news was not well received. It was considered highly improbable that Jesus would come back as a black person, or as a woman, and certainly not as both. Indeed, truth to tell, the Vatican was ill-prepared for a Second Coming, even if the claimant had conformed perfectly to the stereotype of Christ as portrayed in so many of the Vatican's paintings. What's more, as Pope Urban XI had remarked shortly before experiencing an agonising headache, if Jesus had decided to return, surely he would have chosen to make his entrance in the Holy City in Rome, not in London.

Saudi Arabia was less of a problem than Cleveland had expected. The rumour about the identity of Cleveland's adviser had reached the Kingdom through diplomatic channels. Cleveland thought the Crown Prince might baulk at a meeting instigated by someone purporting to be Jesus. To his surprise, Cleveland discovered that Islam agreed with Christianity up to a point, that Jesus would return and destroy the Antichrist, as well as the infidel armies of Gog and Magog, before accepting Muhammad as God's final messenger and converting to Islam. The Crown Prince, an enthusiast for modernising his country, found it amusing that Jesus had returned as a black woman. "If she's Somali, she'll be Sunni," he observed.

By the end of the day, all the G20 countries had agreed to attend the extraordinary meeting. If distance prevented any heads of state from reaching London in time, they agreed to participate through their ambassadors or via video-conferencing facilities.

Preparations for those who could attend in person were frenetic. Several central London hotels cleared their top floors to accommodate the world's leaders and their retinues. When Cleveland objected that the British Government couldn't guarantee the safety of so many of the great and good at such short notice, Jess told him not to concern himself with security. She guaranteed all would be safe – unless they opposed her mission.

25.

In God's image

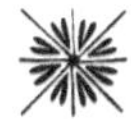

WHILE Cleveland and his office were fully occupied in organising the extraordinary meeting of the G20 for the following day, Jess had been moved to one of the more commodious guest rooms in Chequers. She had been told they would all be heading back to London that evening, but given her evident new-found influence with the Prime Minister, it had been assumed a larger room with a better view would be more appropriate than the more modest accommodation she had been allocated the previous day.

Archie found himself at a loose end. He knocked on the door of Jess's new room. There was no answer. He gently opened the door. Jess was sitting in a chair, apparently staring at a blank wall.

"I'm sorry," said Archie quietly, backing out. "I didn't mean to disturb you."

Jess swung round and said: "You may stay." She indicated that he should sit down in a chair opposite her. "What do you want?"

Her expression was enigmatic. Archie couldn't tell whether she was irritated by his intrusion, or amused, or pleased. She was looking directly at him and once more he felt the power of her gaze. Those green eyes encompassed him. She knew him, his strengths and his weaknesses, the good and the bad, his hopes and fears.

"I had nothing better to do, so I thought we might have a chat," Archie replied defensively.

"You had nothing better to do, so you thought to pass the time in idle chatter with the Scion of the Lord," said Jess.

"No, no," Archie mumbled hurriedly. "I didn't mean that."

"What else could it mean?" Then Jess laughed. "For someone with a reputation for a brilliant mind and a lecherous nature, you seem easily embarrassed."

"I find such a reputation embarrassing," said Archie, recovering his composure. "Actually, I was wondering what you said to James to make him so compliant. I'm not breaking a confidence if I tell you he had serious doubts about your claimed identity."

"He still has doubts. He labours under the burden of a largely secular and wholly materialistic society. But I revealed to him the price he will pay if he allows his scepticism to impede my mission."

"When I came in you were staring at the wall. What were you doing?"

"I was communing with my Father," said Jess.

Archie was silent for a moment. Then he said, "You mean God."

"Excellent," Jess replied. "Well done. You've worked it out."

Archie was hurt. "You've obviously acquired the very human penchant for sarcasm. May I ask what you were communing about?"

"Why not?" Jess replied. "After all, it affects you and all your fellow creatures. I've asked God for an extension. He gave me six days to prove that he shouldn't blow you and the rest of the universe away. I can see now it will take me a little longer. I made a good case. Organising meetings like the G20 takes time, and the changes I need to make to human society will take longer. I asked for three months."

"What did he say?"

"He said no," Jess replied. "He said, *You asked for a week. You have a week. And not one day more.*"

"Oh!" said Archie.

"I didn't really expect Him to agree," Jess said sadly. "Once He's made up His mind, He refuses to change it, whatever you say. Even if He knows He's wrong, He won't admit it."

"He sounds almost human," said Archie.

"That's hardly surprising," said Jess. "After all, you were made in his image."

"But He's God," said Archie, disappointed at what seemed to be God's frailty.

"He's a creator," Jess explained. "He likes to create things. And He's amazingly good at it. He made the entire universe out of next to nothing. But once the creating side of things is done, He stands back and lets things take their course. Then, if things aren't going well, He likes to clear the decks and start again with a new project."

"But you disagree," Archie queried hopefully.

"I don't like to discard something just because it's not perfect. Two thousand years ago, I came to tell Man what he needed to do. To be fair to my Father, he supported me then. We both agreed that Man had done rather well. By then, half a millennium before my first mission, we'd seen Buddhism emerge and the brilliance of the Greeks illuminate the world and we thought you were worth it. I came then with His full approval."

"But you feel it didn't turn out well," said Archie.

"Didn't turn out well!" Jess laughed. "You were supposed to listen to me, not crucify me. You then persecuted those who tried to take my message seriously until the Roman Emperor Constantine attributed his victory in war to me and adopted Christianity as the right religion for the ruthlessly militaristic Roman Empire. Me! The prophet who preached that you should turn the other cheek became the mascot for the most ruthless war machine of the ancient world. Justifiably, my Father and I were a tad disappointed. Since then, there have been ups and downs. You've had endless wars, endemic poverty and environmental hooliganism. The Renaissance was good and the Age of Reason showed real promise, but all in all, it wasn't good enough. In the twentieth century, you had the war to end all wars in which sixteen million died. And then, twenty-one years later, you had a second world war in which anywhere between sixty and eighty-five million died. God gave up on you some time ago. I fought your corner, but it drove a wedge between me and my Father. I have to tell you that my talk with Him before you came in did not end well. His last words to me were, *How sharper than a serpent's tooth it is to have a thankless child."*

"That's King Lear, isn't it?" queried Archie, a little surprised the Almighty would quote the Bard.

"Yes," Jess confirmed. "He's very fond of Shakespeare."

"I thought God looked on us all with the same love and compassion," Archie hazarded.

Jess laughed. "Really? If you've read the Old Testament, you'd know he had a chosen people. He's not now, nor has he ever been, an enthusiast for equality. He's more into merit which, unfortunately for me, is usually measured by the extent of your obedience to his will."

"So He's a fan of Shakespeare?"

"He likes to see his creation doing well, being creative," Jess replied, "but 'fan' is not the right word. He takes credit Himself for all that He thinks is good. And why not? After all, He created Shakespeare."

26.

Questions

FRED Tyler took time out from his preparations for the G20 meeting. He had something else on his mind. He phoned an old friend from his Oxford days. Peter Tullogh now worked in the Oxford Department of Experimental Psychology.

After an exchange of pleasantries, Fred asked a question. "Peter, do you think it's possible for someone to induce severe pain in someone else so that they have no choice but to do as they are told?"

Peter laughed: "Yes, of course. It's called torture. From the old school cane to waterboarding and beyond, Man has frequently used pain to make others obey …"

Fred interrupted. "No, sorry, I didn't make myself

clear. Is it possible to induce pain by non-physical means?"

"You'll need to give me some context," Peter replied. "When you say non-physical, do you mean coercive control? Isolating someone from their friends and family…"

"No," said Fred, embarrassed at his inability to phrase his question clearly but reluctant for obvious reasons to explain the case he had in mind. "Is it possible through some form of induced hysteria to cause someone such physical pain that they are compelled to do what you tell them to do?"

"Like voodoo?" Peter asked brightly.

"Not really, though maybe," Fred replied. He realised that he would have to give the context if he was to have an answer. He would have to tell Peter that the British Prime Minister was now under the control of a black woman who seemed able to induce pain in him, any other world leaders and indeed probably anyone else, if they refused to do her bidding and that she could exercise this power at a distance and on people she had never even met. He realised the absurdity of the question but he was a rational being and he needed a natural explanation for the insanely bizarre situation in which he found himself.

"Let me give you a for-instance," he began. But

before he could utter another word, he felt an agonising pain emanating from just above his left eye and spreading like the mushroom cloud of a nuclear explosion through his whole head. He ended the call.

27.

Orders, Part One

Wednesday

WHEN Jess made her entrance at the Excel London in Newham, there was a universal intake of breath from the assembled world leaders and their entourages. In her brilliant white trouser suit and white leather shoes, she strode onto the platform of the multi-function conference suite as though she owned the entire one-hundred-acre site. The room fell silent.

"Ladies and Gentlemen, I am Jess, and I am here to put mankind on what we will all agree is the right path. You represent the world's most powerful political entities and the wealthiest economies. Therefore I hold you responsible for the parlous state in which I find your planet. You have one chance to prove that you are worthy of the positions you hold, despite your abysmal record to date.

"There are two pressing problems that threaten your world. The first is the damage to your planet; the second is the unfair distribution of its resources.

"I am well aware of the many excuses you have for perpetuating the present system. I am here to tell you that none of them can withstand my scrutiny. You pride yourselves on the power you exercise. But you seem to be impotent when it comes to taking and implementing constructive or innovative decisions. So I am going to tell you what you are going to agree upon and what you are going to do.

"I hear you ask what gives this woman the right to tell us, the most eminent people in the world, how to run the planet? What does she know of the complexities of running a modern, technologically advanced society? Well, I could confirm the rumours that I know are circulating amongst you – that I am the Scion or Daughter of God, the Creator of the universe. But what would be the point? Most of you don't believe in God, so any claim to authority based on his paternity is unlikely to cut much ice with you. Or again I could aver that I am the Second Coming of Jesus, long predicted by both Christianity and Islam. But given the world's rather silly obsession with ethnicity and gender, I'm sure you would object that Jesus was a Jew and male, whereas I, fairly obviously, am neither.

"So why should you pay attention to me? Many of you already know the answer." Her voice now had a hard edge. "Let any who are still in doubt, speak now."

There was complete silence. Too many had already experienced the consequences of offering resistance to this woman's will. And those as yet unscathed had been fully informed of the exquisite pain that assailed those who failed to fall into line.

"Very well," said Jess. "Let's get on with it. You have ten years from today to end your use of fossil fuels. You will divert most of the money you spend on defence into developing alternative sources of energy. After all, your greatest enemy at the moment is climate change. It will be hard and disruptive, but you will do it because failing to do it will be far harder and more disruptive for you. Given your propensity for kicking difficult decisions down the road, you may be hoping that you can delay implementing my orders by bureaucratic procrastination. Not so. Yes, I know God said the sins of the fathers shall be visited upon the children unto the third and fourth generation but that is one of several points on which my Father and I disagree. You, not your children, are going to face the full consequences of your own sins."

There was a murmur of surprise from the audience. Jess answered the unasked questions brusquely.

"It should come as no surprise to anyone who has read the Old and the New Testaments that Yahweh, the God of vengeance amongst other things, and Jesus, the advocate of love, didn't always see eye to eye."

Mario Marino, the representative of the Vatican who had been invited to attend as a courtesy to the Pope, thought of intervening. Any suggestion of a schism between God and someone purporting to be Jesus obviously threatened the "Three in One" concept of the Trinity. On the other hand, as a Jesuit, Mario could see that a separation of God from Jesus, while obviously unthinkable, did resolve the troubling consistencies between the blood and thunder commands of God in the Old Testament and the almost other-worldly selflessness of the teachings of Christ. But then, on the third hand (he was after all a Jesuit), it raised the question of the role of the Holy Spirit. Could it be that the function of the Holy Spirit was to reconcile the differences between God and Christ? He would need time to explore the theological implications. He decided to remain silent.

Jess continued with her list of action points:

"From now on, all those of working age who can work will work. The trend for more and more people of working age to opt for ways of life that are a drain on the economy and their fellow citizens will stop. It is an economic model that is unsustainable. It is also socially corrosive. All who can should contribute to the economy; otherwise society will not be able to sustain a civilised way of life for the young, the old and the infirm.

"Everyone who can, will work from home. Governments will provide adequate grants for every homeworker to convert their home into a satisfactory workplace, thus creating a great number of jobs for builders, designers, equipment suppliers and other service providers. The practice of spending two or three hours a day travelling to and from a workplace when, in many cases, it is entirely unnecessary will end. Home-working will save employers and employees money and will reduce carbon emissions substantially.

"Empty office buildings will be used to meet social and community needs or converted into much-needed residential accommodation under strict regulation to ensure each unit meets all the requirements for good housing, including full provision for home-working. The ground floors of such buildings will be reserved for retail and entertainment facilities to ensure residents have all they need within easy reach.

"People will be allowed only one flight a year for leisure purposes. Business flying will be permitted but will be so expensive that all companies will use teleconferencing whenever possible.

"Within one year all waste must be either compostable or recyclable. That will be a challenge for the packaging industry and their clients, but if another piece of plastic drifts out into the oceans after the six months deadline, the offending companies will forfeit all their assets to their governments. You think it can't be done? Just watch.

"The infrastructure of each country will be developed to meet the changing needs of business and the people. High-speed broadband will be provided to every household. There will be major implications for transport, roads, rail and air travel. The savings on such infrastructure will be invested in maintaining and expanding the electricity grid and developing local amenities in towns and villages with the intention of creating real local communities, not the entirely bogus, notional communities to which your governments so frequently refer when wilfully fragmenting society and distancing themselves from any responsibility for social cohesion."

Jess paused. There was a stunned silence as the audience struggled with the length of her last sentence and the abundant complexity of thought it carried.

"Finally, you will devote sufficient resources to end the burning of fossil fuels. My Father has expressed astonishment and irritation that having blessed your planet with more than adequate provision for energy, you have only recently turned your attention and your technical expertise to developing renewable sources. Each day the Earth receives, in solar radiation alone, ten thousand times the energy it currently consumes. So get on with it. On this, my Father and I are as one.

"There will now be a short break," she concluded, "while you digest what I've said and before I address the problem of the unfair distribution of wealth."

28.

Papal deliberations

POPE Urban XI had responded with mixed feelings to the news that the Second Coming might actually have happened.

Of course, the Church had been waiting more than two thousand years for such a momentous, climactic event. Indeed, in many ways the Second Coming was necessary to make sense of the story of Jesus. Jesus had suffered crucifixion to expiate man's sins and to promise mercy for all sincere penitents, but the unceasing cycle of human lives had to end at some point with a judgement. That judgement was the foretold Second Coming when Jesus would sort out the wheat from the chaff. So at the level of narrative satisfaction, Pope Urban considered

Jess's arrival very good news.

There was another reason for Urban's approval. Although he couldn't admit it, he, like so many others in the Christian clergy had had his doubts from time to time. Did God exist? Was Jesus, reared as the son of a carpenter, truly the Son of God? Had Jesus really risen from the dead? Well, if Jesus had come again, the answer to all these questions must be an emphatic yes. It validated the Bible story beyond question. Now faith, frail in its interminable battle with its implacable enemy doubt, could be relieved of its burden, replaced at last by certainty.

That said, Urban could see some very real problems. Urban, as Pope, was at the head of a global enterprise with immense wealth at its disposal. With this immense wealth it performed good deeds around the world and basked in its status as the most important global Christian benefactor. Nevertheless, Jesus – or Jess – might not be best pleased that a being who had eschewed material wealth was now represented on Earth by one of the world's richest institutions. However much the Catholic Church gave away each year, it still managed to maintain probably the most impressive portfolio of real estate the world had ever seen. It really didn't sit well with the sentiment that it would be easier for a camel to fit through the eye of a needle than for a rich man to enter the Kingdom of Heaven.

And then there was the problem of the moral character of the Church's personnel. For years the foundations of Christ's Church had been rocked by scandal and criminal prosecutions – from paedophilia amongst priests and bishops to financial corruption at the highest levels of the Church's administrators. It had been difficult enough to handle the world's media, but explaining the Church's troubled record to its perfect founder would stretch the intellectual capability and verbal dexterity of the Church's public relations department to, and probably well beyond, breaking point.

So if Jess was indeed the Second Coming of Christ, the outcome for the Church was unlikely to be entirely positive. Urban's people in the Secretariat for Communications in the Roman Curia had already drafted arguments to justify the extraordinary hierarchical, financial, bureaucratic juggernaut that the Church of St Peter, the Catholic Church, had become. "It had been necessary to ensure that the faith was spread and sustained everywhere on the planet. The redistribution of wealth from the rich to the poor required monetary and fiscal competence of a high order. The success of Christianity had required managerial expertise of exceptional quality."

Their defence of the Church's moral record was less persuasive. Even the most glib and oily-tongued apologist would find it difficult to explain, much less excuse, the Crusades (when Pope Urban II had given carte blanche to all and sundry to rape and pillage their way across Europe to the Middle East), the Inquisition (when in an effort to stamp out heresy, heretics were routinely imprisoned, tortured and executed), and the modern scandals of paedophilia and financial corruption which, while not new ecclesiastical sins, had only in recent years been thoroughly and globally exposed.

Paedophilia was the *colpo di grazia*. Given the claim that Catholic priests were the essential intermediary between the faithful and God, the Church's egregious record of sexual abuse of minors constituted perhaps the most heinous of the Church's crimes against both Man and his Creator, and surely to Jesus – or Jess – the least forgivable.

Urban sat back in his favourite chair in his private apartment and tried to pray for guidance. If Jess was truly the Scion of God, the possibility of having to deal with the Second Coming, given the Church's severely tarnished history, filled Urban with trepidation.

All things considered, it would surely be better if this black Somali woman turned out to be a fraud. If Jess was an impostor, surely God would inform the head of

His Church on Earth. But, oddly, God maintained an inscrutable silence. Only two images entered the papal mind and persisted there in a kind of cinematic loop. The first was Jesus ejecting the money-lenders from the temple; the other was Jesus declaring that it would be better for any man who harmed a child "that a millstone were hanged about his neck, and he be cast into the sea, than that he should offend one of these little ones".

When Urban eventually managed to terminate this unwelcome, involuntary repetitive film show, he made a decision. He would not go to meet Jess himself. He was not ready to face her. He would send his trusted adviser, Mario Merino, in his place.

29.

Orders, Part Two

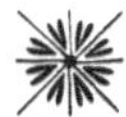

AFTER fifteen minutes, Jess re-entered the chamber and approached the stage. Before she could speak, Marcel Baudelaire, the French Prime Minister, stepped forward and asked if he might have a word.

"Yes, of course," Jess said graciously. "Please join me on the platform and use the microphone so that all can hear what you have to say."

Baudelaire accepted the offer. "I and some of my fellow leaders have briefly discussed your proposals …"

Jess interrupted him. "These are not proposals. They are edicts."

"Yes, yes, of course," Baudelaire said hurriedly. "But even so, there is a problem."

"Which is?" Jess asked with a shard of irritation in her voice.

"The people," said Baudelaire. "The people will not accept such sudden and draconian curtailment of their freedoms. Such abrupt and savage attacks on the people's freedom of movement, on their diet, on their very way of life will be resisted."

"No, they will not," said Jess simply. "All of you here claim to be leaders of men. If you are worthy of such eminent positions, you will, I'm sure, be able to explain to the people that either they accept my edicts or they will suffer far more than the curtailment of some of their freedoms. There will be floods and famine. There will be civil wars and wars between nations. Humanity will turn upon and destroy itself. Given the choice, they will accept my edicts.

"You do not need to tell them that God lost faith in them some time ago and only my intercession has prevented Him from discarding this universe already. But you, the leaders of men, you *do* need to understand that the future of humanity is balanced on the edge of a knife. You are within days of obliteration if you fail to adopt a wholly positive attitude to my plan for your future."

"We will try," said Baudelaire, "but that does not mean we will succeed. People have become increasingly sceptical about their leaders and assertive of their rights. I fear they will not take kindly to such peremptory commands and abrupt diminution of their rights."

"I know this is true," Jess said. "They have become self-obsessed. They have taken the inadequacies of their leaders as good reason to elevate themselves. They need to understand that you have fallen to their level, they have not risen to yours, or rather to the level that leaders need to reach to justify their right to lead. I'm hoping that in these extreme circumstances, you will make a special effort to be untypically worthy of the image you have of yourselves."

This overt insult proved too much for the Chinese ambassador to the UK, Chen Xiaoping, a tall, portly figure, who was standing in for the President of the PRC. "I represent a civilisation that stretches back far beyond your first, not entirely successful, visit to mankind. I question your legitimacy here …"

He was about to elaborate on his point. He would not threaten her. He knew the consequences of such folly. But he intended to explain to this arrogant black woman that the leaders of his country could claim to be enthusiastically endorsed and legitimised by the votes of one and a half billion people. Who was this woman, whatever her provenance, to lecture and mock such an august gathering? That was the line he planned to take, hoping to undermine Jess and at the same time, emphasise the inherent superiority of Chinese civilisation over all others. But he was to be comprehensively disappointed. Abruptly, without any warning, he disappeared. One second he was there, and the next he wasn't. There was no bang, no puff of smoke or haze of mist. Just empty space where Xiaoping had been. The entire audience emitted a synchronised gasp. Then all looked to Jess.

"We really don't have time for this," she said. "I am not here to listen to the blatherings of an apologist for an authoritarian but unstable political system with laughable democratic pretensions. You are shocked when one of you is nihilised. If God has his way, this entire universe will disappear as completely and speedily as the late Chen Xiaoping. You face the existential threat to end all existential threats. This existential threat is to existence itself.

"Please, no more interruptions. I need to give you your second set of instructions for how to arrange a fairer distribution of the world's wealth. I suspect you will find these adjustments even more difficult than the lifestyle changes."

The only sound was the faint murmur of distant traffic.

"First, everyone of working age who can work must work, and everyone who works must earn at least a minimum wage. The minimum wage will be calculated on the basis of what is sufficient for all the basic necessities of life within the economy where people live. It will also be set at a rate at least fifty per cent higher than the maximum benefits paid to the unemployed. Yes, this means the minimum wage for work must be set much higher than is the case currently. Why? Because ensuring there is a substantial gap between living on welfare and what low-paid workers earn is the best way to persuade those at the bottom of the working-age pyramid to work. As there is a limit to which a civilised society can reduce welfare benefits, a substantial increase in the minimum wage is the only answer. Those who through physical or mental disability are unable to contribute should be well cared for and given every help to lead fulfilling lives.

"This reallocation of wealth will be achieved through a global tax. A relatively modest flat rate on all countries of 1.5% of GDP per annum across the board will be more than sufficient to achieve this goal.

"The second and final component of this set of instructions is that after allowing for provision of the minimum wage, the remaining wealth of the world must be distributed in proportion to the hard work, the talent and the contribution to the common good of each individual – that is, on merit. Despite a strong egalitarian strand of thought in humanity, the current system of wealth distribution is grotesquely uneven, as well as profoundly unmeritocratic. I say at once that we have no objection to an uneven distribution of wealth. In fact, we favour it. Both my Father and I are very much committed to a system of judgement based on merit, both in morality and in the distribution of wealth. Those who are good shall find heaven; those who are bad, will not. Those who work hard, show talent and contribute to the common good deserve to be rich while those who are fit but lazy must accept a subsistence level of support because they are an unproductive and uncreative burden on their more industrious fellow citizens. Few right-minded people will argue with the principle of meritarianism.

"That said, devising a fair system based on merit is not as simple as it sounds. Working hard is fairly easy to measure, but the other requirements are more difficult to quantify. For example, under talent I include, amongst other qualities, intelligence, an empathic faculty and the ability to innovate, lead and inspire. We must also take into account required length of training, unsocial hours and adverse work conditions. Finally, we must give due weight to the rules of supply and demand and scarcity.

"Under contribution to the common good, we need to

assess and quantify the contribution of each individual towards the enabling of others to fulfil their potential and enjoy their lives.

"Finally, we must include the approbation of the masses. Although my Father created you, there are aspects of human nature which even He finds difficult to comprehend, but clearly any system of merit to be applied to humanity must take into account humanity's own assessment of value – a kind of bums-on-seats criterion.

"For each of these factors you need scales on which to measure these qualities and weightings to achieve the optimum result. No mean task! You will be pleased to hear that with the help of God (He's exceptionally good at maths), I am able to supply an algorithm that fits the bill. This algorithm must be applied and its remuneration results implemented within the year.

"I realise that a system of wealth distribution based on merit will be disruptive and rather upsetting to many who, without merit, have enjoyed great wealth. Bankers and speculators no doubt will find the adjustment particularly difficult. As we say in heaven, *You can't save a soul without excising the sins from the sinner*. I think you have a similar saying – *You can't make an omelette without breaking eggs*. In this instance, the benefits of this omelette will more than justify excising the shell and beating the contents into submission."

Jess paused, waiting for the gasps of her audience to subside. Throughout her speech, there had been murmurs of surprise, anger and disbelief, but her commands on redistribution of wealth evidently prompted the most concern amongst the great and good. Unperturbed, Jess continued.

"I am leaving with you a form for you to sign. It is a binding declaration that you will implement all the measures I have outlined here today, and that you will implement them within the allocated time periods. Each one of you will sign on behalf of your country. This document will have far more than the force of an international treaty. The penalty for defaulting will be universal annihilation. You have four hours to sign.

"There is one other edict. It's true my Father said *Go forth and multiply*. He should have added *but not exponentially*. I'm not giving specific instruction on this one, but I exhort you to get a grip on it. Make birth control universally available and promote it vigorously. Frankly, eight billion of you is more than enough, and women in Third World countries will appreciate a break from unremitting gestation. If this necessity is too difficult for you, I will lend a hand and drastically reduce the birthrate by economic, psychological and even physiological means, as has already happened in some so-called advanced countries."

As Jess turned to leave the platform Luigi Ferrari, the Italian Prime Minister, stood up: "Excuse me and please don't take offence," he said, mindful of Chen Xiaoping's fate, "but I feel I must ask. Within my country is Vatican City, the beating heart of the Christian Church – your Church. The Church teaches that mechanical and chemical forms of birth control are unacceptable. The Pope in particular feels strongly about this issue."

Jess grunted. "What does the Pope know about children? Tell him this. He should concern himself more with the born than the unborn. Let him who is without sin cast the first stone. Gently remind him about the dangers of being thrown into the sea with a millstone around his neck. And urge him to ease up on claiming that the Vatican is 'the beating heart' of my Church. It would do no harm to point out to him that if he has a role, for now at least, he works for me."

30.

Vatican City

FROM the moment Pope Urban had chosen him as the best man to attend the extraordinary meeting of the G20, Mario Marino, the Pope's emissary, had felt uneasy about his assignment. Jess's dismissal of Italian Prime Minster Ferrari's concerns for papal sensitivities did nothing to assuage his concerns.

At first, on news that someone had appeared making a credible claim to be Jesus, the majority of cardinals thought that the Holy Father himself should travel to London. As the inheritor of St Peter's mantle, God's representative on Earth and the rock on which God's Church had been founded, surely the Pope should have the honour of greeting Jesus on his return.

Those closest to the Holy Father were less sure. First of all, how could they be certain that this woman was not an impostor, a pretender? After all, the world was full of lunatics and fanatics who could be persuaded to believe anything, however absurd. Indeed, if this most recent contender had not already demonstrated miraculous powers, she would have been brutally discounted out of hand as a delusional fraud.

But she had demonstrated miraculous powers. Indeed, by all accounts, she had already performed sufficient miracles to merit beatification, if not canonisation.

Except some of her miracles had clearly involved coercion – and coercion was more commonly associated with evil rather than good. Of course, coercion had its role to play. As a Jesuit, a follower of those who had initiated the Inquisition, Mario Marino would be the first to concede that brute force could be employed as a means of achieving noble ends. But the ends must be truly noble – for example, to save a soul or defend Mother Church.

Were Jess's supernatural accomplishments employed exclusively for good? She obviously thought so, but her certainty was not conclusive. What she proposed would be incalculably disruptive. Reduction in carbon emissions was in hand in parts of the world, but her timetable for a global reduction in carbon emissions was unachievable without economic and social turmoil. The developing economies depended on cheap carbon fuel to industrialise, their only hope of improving the standard of living. This woman was condemning the majority of the world's population to ineluctable poverty.

The first world would face different but no less intractable difficulties. Stipulating people should work from home would almost certainly damage productivity, as would restrictions on national and international mobility. It was at least arguable that Jess's programme was economically dangerous, socially divisive and inexcusably risky – and not therefore indisputably good – not like saving a soul or protecting Mother Church.

That said, it was clear she was not interested in debate. She had issued her instructions and intended to enforce them. It really came down to a simple question. Did she have the power she claimed to possess? She had proved she could inflict pain, but so could mankind. Her powers might be supernatural while human power was more mundane and pedestrian, but human might could inflict indescribable agony on whole cities.

Mario Marino was reviewing options because he had to submit a report to Pope Urban. Although not given a detailed brief, he knew he had questions to answer.

Was the woman Jess truly the Second Coming of Christ or a false prophet? And either way, how could she be contained? That was the word the Pope had used – "contained". As a Jesuit, Mario Marino knew that the word "contained" could cover a multitude of sins.

31.

We have no choice

JESS left the conference suite. As soon as she was out of earshot, the debate began. Was what she ordered possible? How could it be achieved in the time she demanded? Would it work? Was it desirable?

It was James Cleveland who brought the assembled members of the G20 to order. "Such debate is pointless," he declared. "As she said, these are not proposals, they are instructions. And I think we all know what happens to those who fail to follow her instructions. In any case, is she not simply commanding us to do what most of us think should be done? She's identified the two problems with which we've been wrestling and come up with an action plan to deal with them. Is that so bad?"

"But it's her action plan, not ours," objected Baudelaire. "She ignores the obstacles we have to navigate around to achieve our goals. We have to take into account the will of the people. She has no grasp of the democratic process."

"Let's be frank," Cleveland responded. "It's fairly obvious she has a low opinion of us and of the people we represent. She's come to us at this time and in this place because we have failed. If she's right, and I think she is, we've brought the planet to the brink of destruction. If God doesn't blow us away, we will blow ourselves away in the foreseeable future. So you're right. She's obviously not a democrat. But let's be honest, democracy hasn't been very good at taking the necessary hard decisions."

"If she has such a low regard for humanity, why is she bothering to save us?" asked Luigi Ferrari, still smarting from her papalistic rebuke.

"Because for some reason she thinks we're worth saving," James Cleveland replied. "It seems God has given up on us. He's all for discarding this particular creation. But Jess disagrees. She sees something in us that's worth preserving."

"Do you think she's really Jesus?" asked Hank Allbright, standing in for the still indisposed Haywood. He had been uncharacteristically quiet throughout the proceedings, mainly because he realised he would have to either endorse or deny Jess's claims to divinity in the US Bible Belt and he couldn't decide which course offered the best electoral prospects for himself and his party. He was leaning towards denial: "I mean why would Jesus come back as a person of colour and a woman?" It was difficult from his tone to determine which characterisation he found more distasteful. "And why London? Why not Washington or New York?"

"Or Paris?" Baudelaire couldn't resist throwing in.

"What's wrong with London?" asked Cleveland. "Last time he chose Jerusalem, not an obvious choice for launching a global religion. London is a cosmopolitan city with a vibrant cultural life and an international financial service sector second to none. Makes good sense for the twenty-first century. In any case, we're wandering off the point. Whether she's Jesus or not, she has the power to both compel and destroy. We've all experienced evidence that this is so. We have no choice but to do as she says."

32.

What it is to be human

"WOW!" Archie said when Jess joined him in the reception area of the UK's suite of rooms. "I was watching you on the monitor. You told 'em!"

"The next few hours will be critical," said Jess. "If I can't report that I have things moving in the right direction and fast, it'll be game over."

It suddenly struck Archie that she was calmly telling him that shortly he might be no more. He might be "nihilised". He might be dead. "You really mean that God would just wipe us out?" he asked, more in hope than expectation of a denial.

"Good heavens!" said Jess. "Have you only just

understood? You worry me. You're supposed to be intelligent. If *you* can't grasp the situation, what hope is there?"

"Calm down," Archie soothed. "Of course I understand intellectually, but we mere mortals need to process the information emotionally."

"Fine. Take your time. You've got about four hours," Jess replied.

"You're not what I expected Jesus to be like," said Archie. "He talked of love, of kindness, of forgiveness. You know – the Sermon on the Mount – the meek shall inherit the Earth. You just blew away the Chinese ambassador."

"Well, the Sermon on the Mount approach didn't work out so well, did it?" Jess replied. "In any case, you were told the Second Coming would be different. I would come when the world was in turmoil, when mankind faced problems it could not solve, when the people would roar with discontent and when many would lose heart. And I would come this second time with power, and I would come to judge. So it was written. So I have come and that's what I'm doing. I am here to test mankind. God has judged you already. He has seen what you've done to His creation and He fears what you'll do if you survive. I understand His fear and His concerns.

He's also somewhat miffed that so many of you don't believe in Him. So He would be done with you. He is a creator. He will not be burdened with your failure. I have taken your part and argued there is enough good in you – enough promise – to reprieve you. Yes, there is good in you. And that good in you I love. But you must demonstrate that you can take the hard decisions."

Archie was only half listening to the second half of Jess's exegesis. No one could fail to admire this young woman. She was so much at the centre of herself, a whole being, the power and the charisma of a god in human form. And what form! The body of a strong, lithe woman, a fine symmetrical face that radiated light – and those green eyes! And then it struck him. She was extraordinarily desirable.

"Do you know what it's like to be human?" Archie asked.

"I'm here in human form," Jess answered.

"That wasn't my question. Do you know what it's like to be human?"

"I know that your five senses determine how much and how little of the world you know. I know that most of you spend most of your lives satisfying, as best you can, your physical desires. I know that reason and emotion co-exist in your being. I know that good and evil do battle within every one of you. I know that there is a spark of creativity, a spark of God, in each of you, and that most of you are capable of love."

"You still haven't answered my question," Archie persisted. "You have come to judge us. To judge us, you need to know what it is to be human."

"Yes, I know what it is to be human," Jess answered. "That is why I came two thousand years ago. To find out exactly what it was to be human. In both my visits, the first and this my second, I have felt hope, anger and disappointment. I have understood the causes of human stupidity, greed and cruelty. I have felt the inevitable fear and confusion of beings never more than a simple accident away from permanent disability or death – and in the end, in all cases, doomed to die. And I have marvelled at mankind's resilience and its capacity for compassion and love. Yes, I know what it is to be human. That is why I have urged God to give me and you a second chance. And yes, now I am feeling the very human emotion of fear – fear of failing."

Archie fell silent. He was struggling to clarify his feelings for this enigmatic, possibly deluded, but inexplicably powerful woman. Had she been an ordinary woman, he would have desired her. But he realised that his feelings for her, unusually for him, were not at all, as he had first thought, carnal. And that was why he was struggling. It was she who was possessing him. She was encompassing him with her love which, although it embraced all humanity, was nevertheless profoundly personal. For the first time in his life, he felt he had begun to understand the human condition. He reached a conclusion.

He said: "I truly believe you are who you say you are."

33.

Tyler has a thought

FOLLOWING his aborted phone call to Peter Tullogh, Fred Tyler had studied all the papers that his friend had published. Most of Peter's work was irrelevant to Tyler's enquiry but there was enough for Tyler to draw conclusions. The result was not entirely satisfactory. Yes, there were cases where it had been possible to inflict pain at a distance by psychological means. The mind and body had a peculiarly interwoven relationship. Amputees could still feel agonising pain in a non-existent limb. And whether through hypnosis or voodoo, there was a plethora of cases where individuals had been made to feel physical sensations without any discernible physical cause. That said, there was no proven evidence that it was possible to trigger pain in a number of people at different times in different places by psychological means simply because they refused to do as they were told. On the evidence, it was Peter Tullogh's view that the exercise of such power was not entirely impossible but it was extremely unlikely.

Tyler had enjoyed more success with his second line of enquiry, namely, if Jesus did indeed decide to pay mankind a second visit, would it be possible to kill him, or, in this instance, her? MI6 confirmed, probably unnecessarily, that if the target was flesh and blood, they would have no difficulty in despatching it. Indeed, they went further. Even if was a silicone-based life form, they could guarantee comprehensive termination.

Tyler was pleased to receive unambiguous, positive news but still felt uneasy. While Jess was clearly made of flesh and blood, she was not your average agitator. Genuine or deluded, she was convinced she constituted the Second Coming of Jesus. Tyler decided to put in a call to the Archbishop of Canterbury.

Ambrose Fisher had been Archbishop of Canterbury, Primate of all England and Head of the Anglican Communion worldwide for seven years. He had never sought the post. He was sure his continuing struggle with faith issues disqualified him from such an elevated spiritual position. But the Church and the then Prime Minister had not seen his agnosticism as an impediment to his appointment as Head of the Church of England. Indeed, cynics had suggested it was peculiarly appropriate. So that was that and there he was.

Tyler gave much thought to how best to broach the subject with the Archbishop. He could hardly ask, *if Jesus were to come again, would it be possible to kill him?* The rumour that Jess was indeed the Second Coming of Jesus must have reached the Archbishop's ears by now. What did the Archbishop think? Was he of a mind with the Papacy that it was inherently unlikely that Jesus would return as a person of colour of the female gender? In which case, Jess would be in the Archbishop's eyes an impostor. The question, *could you kill an impostor pretending to be Jesus?* was scarcely worth asking. In any case, asking whether it was possible to kill someone – anyone – was inherently problematical, especially if you were the UK's Foreign Secretary and certainly not a question one would normally address to the Archbishop of Canterbury.

On the other hand, Ambrose Fisher might believe Jess truly was the Messiah come a second time, as prophesied in the Bible. He was after all a renowned liberal, having supported female bishops, gay marriage and finally the marriage of any two people, of whatever gender, on the sole condition that they loved each other. He might well feel that the return of Jesus as a black female was more than appropriate for the times we lived in; more, it would probably be an endorsement of his long-held, inclusive non-judgemental position on all issues.

In that case, it would be the height of idiocy, not to mention indiscretion, to let the Archbishop of Canterbury know that a senior member of the British Government was considering an extrajudicial killing. The Archbishop would be horrified even if Tyler explained that there was no other way to re-establish some degree of sanity in UK and world affairs.

The heart of Fred Tyler's problem was simply expressed. Would it be possible to kill Jesus if he came a second time? In short, would the Messiah be killable? If he or she had come to judge mankind, surely mankind would just have to put up with it? Surely it couldn't be a problem that could be solved by a bullet or a car accident or an untraceable poison. Or could it? After all, Jesus had been nailed to a cross the last time. The Romans knew how to deal with dissidents. Perhaps it was as simple as that now.

But when Jesus first came, he refused to exercise political power. This time, Jess had seized it. She had come not to exhort but to command. She must therefore have some form of protection. MI6 could well be wrong. Even if she was flesh and blood, she could be one they couldn't kill.

And then Fred Tyler had a thought that confused, terrified and exhilarated him in one fell swoop. Why had he not been struck down by pain? Those who had only just thought to resist Jess's will had experienced agony. Any who stood against her were blown away. But he had been pondering her assassination and nothing had happened. He had consulted MI6. Nothing had happened to him or to them. Perhaps she had a worse fate planned for him. Or perhaps, and this seemed more likely, she had lost any power she claimed to possess.

He decided to postpone his call to the Archbishop.

34.

Changing the rules

AFTER three hours of listening and contributing to the G20 debate, James Cleveland withdrew, leaving Fred Tyler to represent the UK.

It was already clear that, despite almost universal reservations, all members of the G20 would sign Jess's Declaration. After all, there was no choice. Pain was a compelling argument. And since the alternative to acceptance of the Declaration was immediate obliteration, there was no point in discussing the principle. In any case, most of the G20 leaders could see some merit in the main policy planks that Jess had laid out. She at least had a plan to solve the world's problems, an achievement that had so far eluded the collective intelligence of humanity.

The only question was whether the member states could meet the timetable set out in the Declaration.

When Cleveland reached his suite, Fiona was sitting at a desk in the outer room. "I've got some good news, sir," she said. "Emma phoned while you were in the meeting. The surgeons have given her the all-clear. The cancer's gone completely."

"That's great news," said Cleveland.

"Oh, and Jess is waiting for you in the main room," Fiona added. "I let her in because she seemed agitated."

He walked quickly into the main room.

"I need to talk to you," said Jess. She was obviously distressed. This woman who exuded self-confidence and who had exhibited superpowers that had cowed the world's leaders seemed vulnerable for the first time.

"What is it?" Cleveland asked. He felt nervous.

"He's breaking the agreement," said Jess. "He's changing the rules."

"What does that mean?" Now Cleveland was really worried.

"He's decided that what I am doing is a breach of the original design. He says it's a creational offence and that justifies Him in breaking the agreement."

"I've no idea what you're talking about, but whatever you mean sounds worse than bad to me. Please explain in simple terms."

"God agreed to give me six days to put mankind on a better path, on the path to man's and the planet's salvation. He was sceptical. He favoured instant annihilation, which He said was both just and kinder all round, but He agreed to give me six days."

"And now He's breaking the agreement?" said Cleveland. "How long have we got. The G20 will endorse your Declaration today. You can tell Him that."

"No, it's not the number of days," said Jess. "It's my use of my powers. He says that free choice was an essential part of the original creational design. He is now saying that my blunt use of pain and death to push through my agenda is coercion and that offends the essence of His creation."

"But He must have known you would use your powers when you set out," said Cleveland. "He can't just change the rules now."

"Well, He can and He has," said Jess. "He's made one concession. He's agreed not to annihilate you, whatever you decide. He will just leave you to your fate … unless, and here's the final twist of the knife, unless I ask Him to annihilate you, in which case, He will immediately wipe you out of existence."

"So what exactly are you saying?" Cleveland was

desperately trying to understand the new situation. "Are you no longer able to inflict pain or eliminate those who oppose you?"

"That is so," Jess replied. "He has forbidden me to use that power."

"But the fate of mankind still hangs on your decision. It is up to you to decide if He is to destroy us. If you give him the go-ahead, we're finished. Otherwise, He will leave us to our fate."

"Correct."

"So the only power you have is to tell God to destroy us,"

"That is so," Jess answered. "He's done it again. He knows I would never tell Him to wipe you out. But that is the only power I have."

"Surely you can still use that power to compel us to do your bidding?" suggested Cleveland. "We won't risk annihilation." He needed to understand what Jess could and couldn't do.

"I can threaten you, but it would be an empty threat," said Jess. "I came here to save you, not destroy you. In any case, why would anyone believe me. I can't perform miracles any more. The only miracle I can perform is to erase you and your universe from the mind of creation."

"Well, that's a pretty impressive superpower, to

destroy a universe!" Cleveland observed.

"Except that if I wipe you out, there won't be anyone to impress, will there? And I will have failed, just as I failed last time."

Cleveland felt an urge to console Jess. "You didn't fail last time. You founded the world's largest religion."

Jess bridled. "Really? Do you think I take much pleasure from the Christian Church? They acquired power, which they frequently abused, accumulated wealth, much of which they spent on themselves, endorsed numerous bloody wars, blessing one or even sometimes both sides, and compiled a less than impeccable record in their treatment of children. If they ever read the Sermon on the Mount, then clearly they didn't understand it."

"Don't despair," Cleveland persisted in his consolation. He was in a good and generous mood. Emma was in the clear. And as for Jess, what she wanted mankind to do was right. It was the only way to save the species. Without her forcing them to act, it would be too late. In any case, he liked her and could see she was distraught. "When I left the G20 meeting, they were on the verge of signing your Declaration. Believe it or not, we all agreed with your objectives. Of course, there were reservations about your radical approach and serious misgivings about the timetable, but in our heart of hearts, we all know that what you want us to do has to be done."

Just as Cleveland concluded, the door of his suite burst open and Fred Tyler, accompanied by two strangers, strode in.

"What is going on?" Cleveland demanded. "I'm having a private conversation. And why aren't you in the G20 meeting?"

"Change of plan," said Tyler with his usual bluntness. "I took the opportunity of your absence to give the G20 a little demonstration. I stood up and I argued against the Declaration. I argued vehemently against the Declaration. And then I accused this young woman of being a fraud."

"Are you mad?" Cleveland exploded.

"Not at all," Tyler responded, enjoying every minute. "You see I discovered that our young, black Messiah here, has lost her powers, that is assuming she ever had any. By launching a diatribe against her and surviving, I've managed to convince the rest of the G20 of that. They all expected me to do a Chen Xiaoping and disappear with a bang in a puff of smoke when I let rip. When I didn't, it was game over."

There was a stunned silence which Tyler had no wish

to break. He was savouring his triumph.

"So what is happening at the meeting?" Cleveland asked.

"Well, there's a much-improved atmosphere," said Fred Tyler. "The members are relaxing, chatting away, chilling out, and eager for lunch." He turned to Jess. "You see it's a relief not to be lectured to, hectored and bullied by a well-meaning but deluded, if not demented, young woman."

"Be careful," said Cleveland. "She still has some power."

"No, I don't," said Jess.

"She can, if she so chooses, destroy us all," said Cleveland. Tyler was making Cleveland angry. What's more, he was insulting Jess which, given her claim that she could initiate the obliteration of the universe, seemed a foolish thing to do.

"Really?" Tyler sneered. "So she can't induce even a mild headache but she can destroy the planet! I don't think so. I'm here to arrest her, something we should have done when she first arrived."

The two strangers who had arrived with Tyler moved towards Jess. Jess stood up.

"Is this really necessary," Cleveland asked. "What are you charging her with?"

"Well, now let me see," said Tyler. "There's threatening behaviour, blackmail on a global scale, grievous bodily harm, oh and at least two or three murders. And I suppose we should add 'impersonating the Messiah', although that's probably not a criminal offence. And when we've finished with her, both the Israelis and the Chinese secret services have expressed interest in having a chat with her. Off the top of my head, I'd say she's in even more trouble than last time – and last time, I recall, ended with crucifixion."

"You're making a mistake." Cleveland could see what was happening. The old, failed framework of pre-Jess reality was being reimposed. Jess was now simply a deluded young woman who had broken the law. If he opposed Tyler, he knew exactly what Tyler would do. Tyler would accuse him of being weak and gullible, before triggering a leadership election. He looked at Jess, who shook her head. She was telling him to concede. She was telling him not to worry about her.

"Well, you're wrong about one thing," said Cleveland, addressing Tyler.

"What's that?" asked Tyler.

"Chen Xiaoping didn't disappear with a bang in a puff of smoke. He just disappeared without trace."

35.

What powers!

WHEN the escort had left with Jess under arrest, Cleveland poured himself a whisky. He rarely drank before dinner but this had been an exceptional day. He didn't offer Tyler a glass. "So how do you think this is going to play out?" he asked Tyler.

Before Tyler could answer, Archie Kildare walked in. "I heard the good news about Emma from Fiona," he said.

"Yes," said Cleveland. "It's wonderful."

"What's happened to Jess?" Archie asked. "I just saw her leaving the hotel accompanied by two men. They looked like MI6 to me."

"She's been arrested," said Cleveland simply.

"Really, really?" Archie was amazed. "I thought she

was unarrestable. Who had her arrested?"

"I did," said Tyler.

"Weren't you taking a helluva chance, given what happened to the last man to cross her?"

"She's lost her powers," Cleveland explained, "or at least she's been forbidden to use them. Tyler here found out and decided to close her down."

"And you let him?"

"If she's not who she says she is, she's committed quite a few criminal offences, amongst them murder," said Cleveland.

"If she's not who she says she is, she hasn't committed any offences," Archie returned. "If she's not who she says she is, how on earth did she cause pain in others? How did she kill Chen Xiaoping? There are a hundred witnesses to testify she didn't touch him. Everything she could be accused of can't be her fault because she's been here with us the whole time, under our supervision. Unless, of course, she is who she says she is. In which case, Tyler's taking a helluva risk."

"It seems God has changed the rules and forbidden her to use her powers," said Cleveland.

"What powers!" Tyler exploded. "What bloody powers? Everything that has happened has a reasonable explanation. If you just accept that she's working for an unknown terrorist organisation, it all makes sense, without any supernatural intervention.

"What about the closing down of our Comms and then its restoration?" Archie asked.

"An inside job," Tyler replied without hesitation. "We have a mole. MI5 is already on it. We'll find him or her when we interrogate Jess, if not before."

"And the coercive pain that various world leaders felt?" Archie persisted.

"Mass hysteria!" Tyler replied. "I checked it out with Peter Tullogh at the Oxford Department of Psychology. His research shows that my explanation is unlikely but possible. And possible is good enough for me if the alternative is magic. Once it was known she could inflict pain on anyone who upset her, and it was also known we were taking her seriously, the seed was planted."

"How do you explain the death of the two Israelis sent to kill her?" Cleveland asked.

"That was organised by her people," Tyler answered. "The Israelis are looking into it. It's obvious that she arranged to have them taken out before they reached Chequers."

"And how on earth could she know they were coming to kill her?" Archie interrupted.

"The same way the Israelis knew she planned to kill

Sharon, the same way they knew we were setting out for Chequers the following day and taking Jess with us. The security at Number 10 is about as reliable as a chocolate rifle. It's infested. The place is full of moles and bugs."

"What about Chen Xiaoping?" Archie persisted. "He disappeared at the G20 meeting this morning."

"Haven't you seen what modern conjurors can do?" Tyler replied impatiently. "It's all very clever but it's now considered a very run-of-the-mill illusion."

"Give in," said Cleveland to Archie. "His mind is made up."

"Of course my mind is made up," Tyler barked. "What's your explanation? Jesus has come back, inadvertently as a black woman, and while on a mission to take over the world, exercised supernatural powers which, amazingly, when we might wish to put them to the test, are withdrawn by God. If you take that line, you'll end up in the funny farm in the cell alongside the one being prepared for Jess."

"We don't put the mentally ill in cells any longer," said Archie, "and funny farm is unacceptably derogatory."

"Suit yourself – but not in white," Tyler quipped. "White suits will be what the men who take you away will be wearing and we wouldn't want there to be any confusion."

36.

Endgame

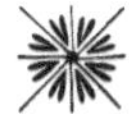

ARCHIE Kildare saw Jess only once more. He had asked Cleveland to arrange for him to visit her and reluctantly MI6 had agreed.

She was being held in a secure house under guard.

"How are you?" he asked.

"I'm fine," Jess replied. She seemed unperturbed. "What did the G20 decide?"

Archie laughed. "They're not very good at making decisions but you did have an impact. They actually issued the Declaration but only after watering down the redistribution of wealth provisions and agreeing a 'more reasonable' timetable."

"Very human," observed Jess, with a smile and a

sparkle in her green eyes.

"What are our chances?" Archie asked.

"Not that good," said Jess. "You need a charismatic human who is a strong leader. It's strange that, with a population approaching eight billion, it's so difficult to find one. I didn't see any at the G20. On the other hand, I've never underestimated human ingenuity so you may yet find a way. God has ruled out any pre-emptive action so you might make it."

"Unless God changes his mind and decides to take us down anyway. No disrespect to your Father but he doesn't seem to be entirely trustworthy."

Jess laughed. "You're right. He's very old and stubborn, and because He makes the rules, He thinks he has the right to change them. And He's an incorrigible hypocrite. He changed the rules this time on the grounds that because I was using coercion, I was undermining free will, a key element in the nature of his creation. Total twaddle. He's used coercion on humankind whenever He's felt like it. What about all those commandments in what you call the Old Testament, with the threat of hellfire and brimstone for those who disobey. It's true, I too was using coercion this time, but I certainly wasn't breaking any of the rules of His creation."

"Nevertheless, you've obeyed him," said Archie. "You

stopped using your powers."

Jess smiled. "It's a father-daughter thing," she said. "But in the end, I always get my way. In any case, the old must give way to the young. He may be immortal but that's one rule He cannot change. He is the past. I am the future."

"Apart from a few references to the Bible, you've fitted in well with our modern times," Archie conceded. "I noticed that you picked up some current colloquial expressions as the days passed. I had to chuckle when you talked of *bums on seats* in your address to the G20. Was that to put us at our ease, or were you becoming more human?"

Jess smiled, a radiant, blazing smile. "I'm more human than you can possibly imagine. I am God made flesh. You need God to fulfil your destiny but – and this is a secret I will share only with you – God Himself needs humanity to be entire and whole. Existence is a joint enterprise, if you like. You are the great hope of His creation. When he gave you free will, he conceded his omnipotence. He took a terrible risk, but it was a risk He had to take to give His creation meaning. It's now up to you to fulfil yourselves and make God complete. I love my Father. Whatever He thinks, He needs you. He needs you to succeed, and that's why I've done all I can to save you."

"Wow!" was all Archie could manage. "I might need

some time to think that through."

Jess smiled again. "Take all the time in the world, however long that may be."

"What's going to happen to you?" Archie asked.

"They intend to hand me over to the Israelis."

"Sounds grim," Archie responded.

"Old habits die hard. But what they intend and what happens are two different things. I think I'll give the Israelis a miss this time round."

"Will I see you again?" Archie felt an overwhelming sense of regret, of grief.

"Of course you will," Jess replied. "In this life or the next. I still have work to do here, so it's quite likely our paths will cross again. Keep an eye out for me. And when my work here is done, I look forward to meeting you again."

"I have to go now," said Archie. "They allowed me only a few minutes. Do you have a message for James? He and I believed in you – do believe in you – not absolutely, you understand, not without some minor reservations, more questions really, but pretty much."

"Enough," Jess said with a laugh. "Just tell Cleveland congratulations from me. And Archie, please make sure they look after my horse."

oooOooo

The following day an Israeli aircraft took off from RAF Benson with Jess and two Israeli intelligence officers. When the seatbelt light went off, the intelligence officer on Jess's left said: "Here we go again. This must seem like old times."

The second officer, on Jess's right, rebuked his colleague: "Leave it alone. She's either deluded or she's the real thing. Either way, there's no need to make fun of her."

"You're very kind," Jess intervened. "But it's only fair to tell you upfront that I'm not making promises to either of you this time round."

Mid-flight, somewhere over the eastern Mediterranean, the plane disappeared. There was no distress signal and flying conditions were excellent. Despite an extensive search, no trace was ever found of the plane, its crew or its passengers.

oooOooo

Three weeks later, Fred Tyler went down with the new virus. He had picked it up from one of the MI6 bodyguards who had recently been working undercover in Iran. The infected bodyguard had been liaising with an Iranian double agent who had been close to the late Ayatollah Muhammad Abbas. After a short illness and despite the best medical attention, Tyler passed away. He had been a difficult patient, giving the nursing staff a hard time. His last words were "Goddam that bloody woman!" (which upset the ICU nurse who had been patiently caring for him), followed by "I can't believe …", at which point he ceased to speak or breathe.

There was some speculation amongst the ICU staff as to how Fred would have completed his last sentence. Most thought he intended to say "I can't believe it", the "it" being his imminent demise as the result of an Iranian bug. Others thought he might have been referring to Jess, as in "I can't believe how much trouble that bloody woman's caused", in which case he might simply have been reiterating his view that Jess was an impostor or, less likely, expressing astonishment at the realisation that she was not an impostor and that, irritated by his intransigent scepticism, she had wrought a terrible revenge on him. The nurse who had been caring for him thought he had already finished his sentence before he died and that given his general negativity, he was simply reaffirming his inability to believe in anything.

Obviously, no one will ever know for sure. Nor does it matter. Only Fred heard the soft, low melodious laughter that seemed to envelop him as he breathed his last. And although the sound seemed profoundly real and not at all unpleasant, he remained convinced that he was imagining it.

oooOooo

Six weeks later, Cleveland was in his office in No. 10 chatting with Archie.

"I've just realised something," said Archie. "Jess is Jesus without the 'u'. I suppose everyone else noticed but it's only just struck me."

"Obviously not as bright as you think you are," said Cleveland.

Fiona buzzed him. "It's your wife," she said.

Cleveland took the call. "Is everything alright?" he asked.

"It's a little more than alright," Emma said. "Brace yourself. You're going to be a father."

oooOooo

In the Vatican, the Pope wept. Someone had hacked the Vatican Bank, a private bank previously believed to be absolutely secure in the heart of Vatican City. The hacker or hackers unknown had scooped out five billion euros. The Church failed to recover the money or its reputation.

oooOooo

What of humanity? Well, if you're reading this, the universe has not yet been blown away. What are our prospects? It's not for me to judge. What do you think? The answer is important. If what Jess said is true, that the universe is a joint enterprise between God and humanity, then everything depends on the answer.

9 781739 547233